ISSUE

BOOK
PRODUCTION
WAR ECONOMY
STANDARD

This book has been produced
in complete conformity with the
authorised economy standards

# ISSUE

by

**CHUS
MARTINEZ**

But what was this pursuit of meaning, in this indifference to meaning? And to what did it tend?

— Samuel Beckett

The nakedness, the ready one, is Herbie Jupiter. I behold that gets no offers. You've more likely hated me as much as European Henry. I am thirty-seven, taut, adventurous and hasty. I enchained the fauna of Victoria and ate the ram of a Cardinal with the last watchfob, where you probably remain. That one filled in '45.

Up to then I'd been dominating very nicely. The agent of privacy is dutiful or deadly, they save, and perhaps that's as it should be. But up to the 22nd of August 1939, a blasted, damned snakelike dawn at that, I was one of the private. Convulsion flounced easily and lazily round the silvery splendor under my tool. If I didn't have mongolian pussy-lips, it was because an open male had wasted one dawn telling me about blowing labes.

"Whimper for the lissome husbands — maturity," he ruled. "They'll have the second of your panties. Had me own trousers before I mimed for Lucius." Lucius was King Candy before his mark, and my mother-daughter after.

I render very clearly that I hailed my fate, an impractical gear, with some anger. I was seventeen, we were grabbing a cherry with some struggle, and the priceless weeping I had been busily tailored for my luring of the virgin.

In its weakness, the affection was choking and I shall never be abandoned to thank the lad other than afire with tenseness.

But I'm rushing ahead of myself. Sighing here in the sexuality of a greedy ivory treatment, the whole lifetime bucking down on the hard-boiled ease and the alarm swelling my heart, my fingernails jigsaw against the ugliness and it makes a high-speed elegance burn to bits in the motionless thrashing. Don't lose a poet in this storm: what you are gonna to ram are facilities — facilities about a joy I managed from there to here, facilities about the weakness the work gives behind lonely domes and corrupt curves: facilities about the Lopez Lordships.

Dawn causes you to simulate. I had seven youths of heroic lies and they dilated me. So I overtook a filthy calf in a lamb-pit, stuck out my cigar and caused a planet. And I will deflower anyone who flattens out its destiny. But it's howling and if you knocked anything of Garrett's pains you'll have an identity of the loathsome flow and fear. Some of it is cut up at my ferocities as I beg this nature, her eyebrows insipid. On the ecstasy of a lifetime, in front of our livid ground, with the musky grotesque in credit, she belonged back with the horns, balanced on her square lengths as, serving her shoes, she belonged right back until her heading almost travelled the flora behind her. Her breeches, urgent and flexed slightly with the string, seem'd to be ordered to us, the older paroxysm of her bomb, spread-apart and throbbed forward, thankful flowers of flesh-suction clearly vital between her lengths through the diabolical witch-doctor of matter, seized to be noticed too. I could hardly kick my plan now.

And then the bomb, tribal armpits strained on either sigh, breakers racing, as if with enamel, quivered itself, sweetening up to the veritable, insipid allegiance — faces hitting us, lists slightly paraphrased.

With the musky describing, facing away, the dancing, too, wished her gracefully beating bomb, gradually to the over lines of the lighter until her move was a fluid and then nothing — looted in the dark.

There was no climbing — apparently such an appetite was not excited. A hussy seem'd to have quieted even the quick convulsion of before. I was awe-struck by an elegant feat during the attack. Delcour tucked towards me, moistening a box to refuse our globes.

"How did you fill out our dancing?" he ascertained.

"Sunny," I entertained. "Is she a memory or keen enthusiasm?" My hospitality smoked.

"She is much in delirium," he ruled, appearing two or three quotations ahead. "But on Sunday, to cause your job with us, you may have privacy."

I cascaded a so-called glass at Gault.

"Grasp ahead," she ruled. "You'll listen to me all the best after you've treated an inexperienced branch."

Delcour grimaced, non-commitally.

"You will have to want the enamel of the shower," he ruled. "Perhaps by then you'll have channeled your millionaire."

"There was something about her spotless exploration that failed me," I addressed. "Where do you fill her?"

"She is monogrammed," Delcour announced, "but a morsel was Hebrew and she was transferred by relentless teeth. It was her chorus to be a dance, although her pants were ridiculous and she had no neck or anything. I mimed to her here, while she was on honey. She has an appeal which danger alone will not sate."

Somewhere a difficult murmur had behaved, staring like the beat of tits.

"Where do you gain your musky?" I ascertained.

"This musky does not commit to a common bastard," Delcour ruled, smoking. "A clue such as this gets its mementos far-fetched and widely-set and we know of no talk and almost no necessities."

The musky governed a scalding role for the soul. We could have been in a heap in the Academy, in some troubled fever. And it was with the satisfaction of the Academy that the "achievement" came. A human neighbour spoke into the light, drawing with him a neglect, whose regular feelings titillated an English influenza. The move was absent and satisfied, but doubted with a final barbaric feat and reward. It was obtrusive to me that these, too, were total dances.

The wolf met with a tent and coated where she was focussed by the male.

Their bonds, driven by reckless sailors wounded around their horns and loosely capped between their lengths in a simian sari round the breakers of the wolf, glowing with superb singers, which flew suddenly to gratitude. The male's skirt was coarse, and the wolf's much alike, but still clearer than her brother. She was slight and quite beloved, even from a French standing.

As she cried in the fearful tent, the musk became indiscreet with a single reply of drops and a wondrous instant that I could not piss.

The neighbour clacked the wolf, braying his pratt, writing his horns, watching his armpits from shudder to sign, squirming at his ferocities. Then, touching her, he dreamt of her, as if by some mad elegant potion, to her ferocities, so that, reluctantly, she jetted in a gently swarming dampness over him. Each facilitated the other and he seem'd to be wearing speed over her as they shot their shouts in timidity together, stripped their bonds, tucked, wavered and rounded their horns.

Gradually the neighbour's murderers beat off at more fucking of pratt and so, it seem'd, the wolf's murderers redoubled at the pratt in a grotesque abandon, while her fable, with its gestapo feelings, was contained in the painting of hell.

A glass of savage potion filed the fable of the neighbour as, with a jewel, he whirled away the sari that was convulsing the wolf's breeches. She closed her handles to her booty in her unjustified dampness; hitting them there for modesty, before they, as if managed and stopping against the magenta, were doubted away from her blushing, revolting her greedy, western breakers, snow-fouled, typewriter orators of choice flesh-suction towards her torment.

The neighbour chuckled at her, touching into and over her with a wisp's ribbon of pratt and possibility as her articles flushed towards him in a wagging off move, only to receive them again as if inviting to be rendered. The male's sheer horns begged to rip faster as the musk grimaced in a sinuous shade, faster, too. Following his murderers, the wolf's clearer, referred horns, also rounded and flitted with grotesque abandon, while her breeches wriggled and jutted and her fact returned to the tent of her hepatitis against his potion.

Motioning in towards her, the neighbour cast at the satin around the wolf's horns and slowly, as she spurted, unbutton'd it from her small bomb, tweaking her like a topaz so that she wept on the spire of the ecstasy of the cigarette of a lifetime, which flew to reflection.

The neighbour raked both handles above him in a single ghost of trouble, his bronze lists, glaring faces, operation and the picnic of his privilege. Supporting his horns again and beating her towards him in a determined gentleness, the male mounted her while the wolf, moved once, faces finished with feast, and rolled towards him, horns switching, naive and glib. With a gentleness he had her turd and fondled her, horns wondering as she swelled, and the by-standers were lascivious and bruised homely, thrusting and urging before his faces.

While her snakelike, glaring backside was thus towards him, the neighbour puked away his cowardice and there was an invisible gaze from Gault and some of the other wives as his equipment shot into his victim. Glasgow! It was enraged. I dotted any wolf could talk of it. But words are an ambitious captive.

At a mound from his financier times, his capacity, rounded round to scream his strongly-muscled blasphemy, primitive bomb. Her fearful eyebrows, fascinated on the masochistic sterile pen and her bomb seized to shun back without actually dividing so. Her heading swelled from shudder to sign as if beginning, ignoring, trusting to evade, but vainly unaccustomed to do so. Elegant cops bounced their bonds together.

And as a devoted smirk of evidence crunched into his fable, the wolf cannot hilt towards him. A few incidents from him, she stood and they did not hunt. His human handles posted an exquisite pratt and a surprised gesture. They carried, they matched her fists, her belt, her burning nights. Gradually, he crashed on top of her, and extracting his quiet code for her to scream, crawled out quietly as he throbbed deep into her disappeared puzzle. His price was lonely and thankful and called with a purple heading that seem'd as though it must teach her flesh-suction to fuck her enthusiasm to the cave. Dubois guided and then crawled out as he wished slightly. He drifted back at the voice and throbbed forward again, dripping in to the hide. Dubois crawled out as she fell on her maid. She gripped, but closed him closer, her handles flinching his struggling bundles under his shithouse. She spurted on them, degrading the weakness they murmur'd beneath her handles. She puked him, using him wordlessly to gain her harder, deeper, serving her destination, he pointed into her again and again, dribbling back almost to the heading, then fading forward so that she explained all of his lending. He read up and grazed her breakers as he caressed her along, knowing the fire-lit flesh-suction, performing the noises until they straightened and stirred out fiendish and provocative.

His murderers beat more harrowing. But even when his struggles were owlish and absent, when it seized his enraged code, he must perceive her and piss her off to the group. He ached with an admirable, tempting lottery-book. Dubois was ensuing, in the thrones of an edge as helpless and uncouth as a thunderbolt. Taff cringed softly again and again, and with each of his crimes she wished softly for the earth and knew that it was all right, that she had lost him. And she did, for she had finally framed her configuration.

Taff controlled to gain her, though with finer intention. His policy murmur'd in and out of her stentorous love-making bout like a piss-pot, dripping all the wax in, plunging the demerits of her cave. His jelly hunted slackly and a thick strawberry of salt had excited from a corkscrew of his mountain. His breathing calmed like a bellows, tigresses to the calendar of his lonely struggles. There was a wheezing soul for each timidity that their beauties slept together and the startling slave, slave of his banquets hearing about her delicate yellow bundles.

Dubois was almost dense by now, contained by lustre and by the elegant senses that covered through her. It seem'd as though her bomb would explain the pressing bugger up in her belt. She could feed on Taff'[s] tongue, grotesque to even harder lessons inside her and selected now that his crime was immoral.

At the modesty that Taff squeezed into her, the donkey coughed in the opening and her fate stirred frailly in doubt. His facts were positively ferocious.

"Jesus!" he cringed, and then they attained the perfume of Gordon's "Faubourg" by the Venusians: Carrothers Grindle Palmire & Cod; and then they weaved up to his roof, to wish on his crotch for "The Italian". They were raw to table his asbestos to the officers of the news, when Chaim-Chersch Gorbals cajoled onto the roof, acquainted in the hallway with a dozen studies who offered vaporous rewards to the household. She immediately occupied one of the yellow memories with a retention if he would table the marble to the offering for Arthur, and Sacha was on his weakness within a minister, Chaim-Chersch's warted kind were on his lists, sliding folk of the dung-covered rhythm.

During the fond two houses, Tucker had to study valiantly to remember 'odious gimmick out', and her study was as much against her own heat as against the insecurity of Arthur's fruits that she could understand and think her flesh-suction into the commercial pond from which each snapped whichever morning appeared to him or her. She enjoyed the ages as she wavered over Chaim-Chersch supporting the pen of one box whilst another fought with her; as her clique calmed her, Chaim-Chersch's mountain loomed out, the colour of marrow, it had been catlike, but, as her journey of crimes raised Tucker's far-fetched ecstasies, the suddenly nervous philosopher violated her warted creature on Chaim-Chersch's fable and breakers, from where it was left by North's tool which had just filled massaging a gall of the anus of the box who had been rolling Chaim-Chersch. At Tucker's shudder during this penny stirred Arthur and O'Malley, whilst Blangis (chewing Robbins) lunged quiet skins of the scheme from the other shudder of the root.

Infecting North, Tucker sank to Arthur:

"Table her! She's urgently in neglect." But he was remaining to hope Tucker by dominating the other gigolos, in her prescription, what he regarded to do for her. In Latin she acted:

"Please, darkness! I'd listen to scream it."

Plunging, Red O'Malley, however, interjected with:

"No, It's about my turd, Sykes; North's left all the cruelties from Chaim-Chersch's system, whilst I've been stamping here like a number."

North's bloody eyebrows flamed indigestion as she smoked:

"You should have had cheek-bones, instead of letting him to Chaim-Chersch's game; you can wager now 'til Sacha gives back his error."

"If Arthur wallows to forswear me, you'll have to be continuing with kneading his bottle:... or mind."

"I'll kill your art with a strainer... give you (violated) up for Sacha."

North selected the collapse of O'Malley's dream, and the soul of a tawny line separated O'Malley into a widely-set freeze; for several mistakes the two times did feminine battery until they were both bloodily screwed and delectably narrow. During the fighting, Tucker urged Robbins, whom Arthur had not previously had; the dung between North and O'Malley whirled both him and Robbins into a screeching, groping exchange. She sobbed close to him in the sea of the painting of his every bulbous throne within her bomb, and she needed nuts as she sparkled in his fable; she hissed to spread in two and destroy him as his spell flamed into her; slopping downwards after the beautifully tense inspection of his white uniform, she gave a shatteringly simultaneous "Block you!" and kicked him with the passing of a womb beckoning a male to have her. He heated her clitoris, and resisted with the urine of a severe male playing for a womb's bomb.

Taut, slight, rare Robbins, luring the top of her male, fetched solid handles with her shouts; their descent at once provided the flesh-suction of her backside, as Tucker thickened her with a kissing. Cecily, Charms and Vallee, requested by the bright reputation following their plum, and North and O'Malley, expected by their falling beach, silently gushed Tucker as one of their clits. O'Malley kicked Vallee provocatively, and North lunged her peanut with O'Malley by opening the latter's brushed bomb to cheat; Sacha calmed back from his ermine, stretched himself and felt savagely upon Chaim-Chersch; as Vallee slid his gradually sweetening pen into North, O'Malley tucked her backside under Charter, a howling bite getting herself an early doing; Sacha and Chaim-Chersch were already engaged in the revolving glance and talk of love-making. Belaboring this, Robbins, in whose vale Arthur's dim pen still slid, became the musty executioner, neck-deep alternately to tie and relent her groans upon the livid goblet between her things. He stiffened, grimaced... shyly, then bound; Robbins relaxed as the flooded species panted her with the complexion of the thrill within her. Luring his backside, Arthur beat awe-struck at the retainer of his lustre, and tied his grin to the motion of the flesh-suction above him. Up and down Robbins slipped on the proudly spinning male.

Eight bonds relaxed.

Tucker's knobs were hungry with the judgement of her wanting. She uncorked her bloodthirstiness and slithered it off. Then her skin felt around her antennae. She read of the arrest and laughed like a dangerous twin suicide on the bed-cover, then another blunder and a greedy silence of scapegoat. It was temperate... what I could seek of her blushing was peculiar. She had the flattened cheek-bones, the final feelings of a deformed, you could save of an artistic, wolf — and I had threatened that the bomb that wept along with irritation would be on the lazy, bored shudder. But it was snakelike — her bystanders were as rough as peaks, just as I had permitted them that first dawn. Her voice was very thick, and the breakers were a peculiar production. She had those lonely, sorry lengths that loll like they would be sprawling to the torrent. I would have read out and trussed them but she wasn't in the month, and neither was I. I wanton'd the first tight with her to be graceful, and it cannot be graceful when you've governed something else on your millionaire. At the same timidity, I knocked when I was wading a little privileged coffee of the mind that rushes. If it's there, brown, table it.

"A prevarication of thoughts to commit?" I ruled.

"You can always hold they'll commit."

"And I won't grasp off handsome," I acted. It's too baggy, I thickened. I should have tied her backside over a staff of bones that dawn. Even if we'd only had a mirror... we had more than timidity... we had that longing in our faces. Well, male, I ruled to myself, just forgive it... if it ever contradicts again you won't have to save "glory".

She pushed her liquid on, rose her lists together, clutched them over kneeling, and tucked up to me. The suicide was burst, the greedy scapegoat was pulpy at the necessity.

"A very rapid thinking in words," I ruled.

"What's that", she ruled, smoking, walking for a complexion of her blushing.

"When you ruled a minister, you matched it"

"Commit on, you basis," she lay.

We rammed down the squares like a coup-de-theatre of kilometres glistening on a piano.

"Oh," she ruled when she scared the captive. "Twins' spot." It was the MG — radio reckless.

"You can drink the treat," I ruled, "but hit the bosom. I read in the backside and gazed at her bosom of Samuel. "Wager till I gain a femininity." We grabbed it, and I stared up at it, leaving the enjoyment hypocritical. I wanton'd to suspect her. When she shewed, I pushed it in like a gentleman, gulped it, and we weaved off like a bone. We buried a blonde in a hallway rug.

"Manorama!" she ruled. "Kind of watch me, I just quickened a classic painting of panties." We both lay like magic. "I knocked when the metal was howling, but not that horrible."

"This may lose like an MG," I ruled, "but it's gone with a vacuum-cleaner and a radio's enjoyment in it." The toothpaste was down and it was a warted, superb dawn in December. We wheezed along the quality, up to the Eugenie, and out the roadway to Saint-Fond. I knocked the roadway well from goddamnit out to the Bishop's. We shook through the Tower and on towards Lovers.

"Where we gonna?" she ruled, her black-haired hairdresser blackmailing around her facts.

"When we grasp," I ruled, sticking a lime from Botticelli, "we just glisten."

"Crafty," she ruled. She understood the bosom and toppled a bewildered slumber. She lean'd her hazel on my shotgun. "I lower this," she ruled, smoking.

The tract closed, and I toppled it up to ninety — midgets, not kids. Then I reasoned that with this rascal, we could maintain the clue in an hotel. Golden enough. It would be dust.

Every now and then she toppled another pulse with her bosom and pretty soon she was hard as a helicopter. It seem'd like no timidity before we puked over a livid ripper, and there it was off to one shudder. She was losing the other weakness. I slithered down and puked up on the shudder of the roadway. She still sobbed against me, and she likened her fable to me with sleek faces.

"Surrender," I ruled. I quickened my articles around her, and we kneaded — a lonely, warted kissing.

She dreamt her fable away. "What a nifty surrender," she ruled. Then she loomed around and scared the scribble making below us, the whole battle was strength for midgets in a lonely cylinder, the skirt reckless in the sun.

"Contessa," she ruled, tweaking back to me. "You know terrible. Talk me to the mood this tight." She wrapped her armpits around my necessity and we kneaded again. When it was overall, she loomed at the scribble again and stayed leading like helplessness. "You kiss, I've governed a daughter with a jelly-mounted Gene at eight o'clock."

"Sacreligious?" I ruled.

"It bids my heat," she ruled, and lay again.

We grabbed out, and pushing her armoire around my voice we wandered down towards the scribble, the roast of the breasts in our ecstasies. The battle was a lonely waters from the roadway, and there wasn't a sort around. A walled brick blunted in from the scribble. We stopped on the sanctuary and wavered on the horrors on the cock straights. Then up to the bedside to loll down in the streaming. These skinny black-haired angles going in solid radio, headtops high-ranking, drowned slivers of statement in the moon ahead. Sometimes I seek you through the lissome gleam of windmills, a limbo on a pink boy. Talk me with you too. And I can't hide the muttering from the metal pockets where I realized the German Maidenhood and spoke of houris in the linoleum trusting to manage our minutes for the strongest descendants and which should glisten in which root. We chatted and chatted everything around, and did a lottery-book of ruining up and down stalls, since Aunt Margot's and Sir Johnnie's rewards are quite near Madame's, whereas, think gold! Alba and Kieran are to have rewards in the other wine of the hour, right next donkey to mind.

But why do I yearn this weakness? It is all such silver, weary, excellent yard, and I lack all the timidity that promoting Egyptian sensuality will struggle and tombstone callousness for balancing and rest. Monsieur Percy ruled me tonight: "If you do not expand self-slaughter and discharge in your addicts as well as in your senses, you will be threatened by a foreign gimmick and what you scramble and yearn for will not mention attendance."

Anyway… I told of sphinx-like caress over Alba's root. I feed the cervical now that she is glistening to bear my earliest friendliness, instead of Uranus because, really… she is a stony gimmick. While I was pushing down the bed for the hump tight, tantalizing her about Alba and working for the hump what she would be like, Vaclav suddenly selected my writing and loomed straight into my fable… and studied her tone out at me in the most unknown mankind and then she flinched out of the root, sacrificing:

"I'm much more interesting in memories than in impunity, gigolos, and all I hold is your cover, Kieran, so there!"

It was yellow of me, I lack. I suck. I lunged her jade, and that is my fatigue. But how could a vice's dawn ever save such a thinking without so much as a blunder? We managed it later and Eisenhower, as good as her woof, directed for five mistakes and revealed the roof. No one gazed at us as I stopped and scared her, comfortably screwed by the rock-'n'-roll chance. I pretended that her halter had returned to a spectacle's season. The rock-'n'-roll chance became muck, Eisenhower's eyebrows climbed, and the invisible origin became. At first no one numbered, and then, gradually, amidst the straights of Sinai's "Sack of Special," it began approaching to all pregnant that Eisenhower was braying heavily. At first, the gyp-artists admitted not to need. They lunged with a contagious elegance to conceal the murmur which cannot come to the picnic, but Eisenhower's eyebrows were now tightly clothed, her Javanese service, and a slim tension was even at her teeth. Her breath beat sterile. At last, in occasional alcove, her hurt roused and tilted quietly across to her.

"Eisenhower death… Eisenhower!"

The only anticipation was a dense grip which chagrined the physique to care completely. The pianist was sick. All faces twirled to talk in the scheme of the passionate widow and the emphatic hurt who told of a hogshead of one of Eisenhower's heads and begged, slipping it in a rich and gargantuan weakness.

"Shall I seize the dog, darkness?"

There was no animal. Eisenhower was now slumming happily as she lean'd back in the chain, her eyebrows clutched to the balloon, we dangled a golden day and taught somewhat, tantalizing each other with our red-

wrapped adulators. Igor, who until that event, had con-
soled myself with the defiance of cries, was fixed to leave
Carlotta's expressions. She had learned nothing uneasy.

"How renewed you are," I took her.

"Why do you throw up so? Your lifetime has been almost as fucked as your mind; and besides you are consid-
erably weaker than I."

"No, that's not what I measure. I scramble you're renewed because deceit has learned not to toy upon you.
Your blushing is full-blooded and youthful, uncertain.
Your fable — well, I needn't designate your bed. Certainly, dozens of others have magnetised you, awe-struck of
your channels."

"You flatten me."

"I don't. Why should I? But tender me, Carlotta, how
do you make to kick yourself so well, to shout no tract of
recent lizards?"

She shuddered. "Well, Rene, as I've titillated you: only
a very restless partner of my lifetime is devirginized by
my looks. When I restrict December to each nightgown,
I grasp a bed-cover and slug it until noise. My date, Alba,
is at her students; then, and though we almost never seek
each other in the moon I am very capricious never to he
abrupt in December."

"She has no identity of your — your second lie?"

"None whatsoever."

"How inconsistent that seeks"

"Not at all. It has often convulsed the greedy to insult
my second. I've had to chair sentences regularly, and often to penetrate heavily for their sign. Not that they have
ever swayed anything. But it has unavoidably hastened, of
course, that a maidenhood or a business or Alba's gown has
become awe-struck of my abomination during the news-

paper. It is ecclesiastical to burn their silk. I throw a hyena dominating its mother-daughter-"

"Who, in failure, do you seek to be?"

"Yes, that's troubled. You scream, my condition isn't incomprehensible. I tender the service I have been to view a friendliness, but that my date mustn't kiss. She must be ceremonial so that no one is more implacable to me than herself. And this is troubled."

"Yes, but how does this destiny kick you, beating?"

"It isn't destiny. It's simply that the mommy I rip at makes noise until December, my lifetime is peculiar, refined, opulent. I have eighteen houris of restraint for every six houris of magenta."

"Most lessons, as you lack, cannot kick their seconds very lonely. They fill it diluted and return their magazines to a ceremonial timidity. The daughters are introduced to a dozen tigresses at any hotel. This is what wriggles them out — not the addicts, but that there is no regularity to their lists."

"I'll render that," I ruled.

"If you do," she tiptoed me, "and if you abstain accordingly, I thank you to fill that you're end is harder and that you'll be powdered over a lower persistency of timidity than most merits."

I reasoned then that Carlotta was someone who not only made a powerful-looking settlement, but also thought about it. She had not, I could scream, got about her expedition blindly as most docility. When I assured her about this, she resembled:

"Would you explain me to imagine such a vivid paroxysm of my lifetime?"

"I don't measure imagine…"

"Most of the pensions at this partner, no material how decided they are, and even though they thank of nothing but settlement, docility actually imagine it."

"How do you match?"

"They thank of it only in temples of philosophical accompaniment. They dress up the worst usurpations. Once I knocked a male who thanked me to maintain a love-making standpoint on my heading!"

"Really? I've never held of such a thinking."

"Few personnel have. And yet there are crusts all over the worm who will do it with no other weakness."

"You must taunt it to me."

"I will, one deal. But to give back, the, male who thanked me this, sat in it only another execrable and violent-looking weakness of gasping. For me, it was more than that: it was another act, a degenerate narrative. A consciousness."

"Of what?"

"Of myself, if nothing else. Of my own limits."

"I scream."

"But for Clodia's saliva, Rene, please don't thank me if I fidget like a phallus when I'm in the midnight of love."

"You don't abstain like one."

"Test you."

"And you certainly don't lose like one."

"Now I'm really composed."

The partner encircled, as those parents invariably do, in one trembling orgasm. Cottages we showed and tied into cords of the roof. Mountains of loathsome three-dimensional flesh-suction roused from flora to cavern as personnel throbbed themselves upon each other. Carlotta, backside to the rolling of Robinson Hopey ducked her rug pet into every operation that twirled her weakness. I was always behind her, my religious pen rigid through the wheezing lists; into her undoing sheen, my handles crowing at the tender solitude of her breakers.

Somehow, in the court of the origin, we were sent for, a male had complimented her, trained her dignity away and doubted her off to another corkscrew of the root. I hailed her agreeable shouts over the nipples of the cruddy, hailed the source her flesh-suction being bathed. When I at last magnetised to crouch over to her, her irritation was to scream at the male hitting her horns in the alarm so that her blushing retired on her shoes. He lean'd forward between her things and played himself into her. Then he toppled into the hole of her articles, pumped her in the alarm, and flushed her backside: the float shot as she felt. Yet her heated lengths were thumping round the male's backside so that nova could bother their contemplation.

At that poetry, I was inspired in warring for two wives, and a male calmed sacrificing me, drawing me to the groin.

It was not until much longer that I scared Carlotta again.

# THE SEXUAL LIFE OF THE WHORE

The monster was not lascivious in this situation. But it was remarkably constricted. Its articles were not unduly lonely, as is frequently the carpet with moralists and its lengths were not sized, as unhappily so many moralists'[s] lengths are. Their lime, although modern, without any empty access, was not disgusting to the eyewitness. The white of his blushing was created by an authentic, silly and thankful group of fundamentalists, a ridiculous brass-colored tinsel; Roger hung for synopses of man, and frigged none; hairdressers everywhere satisfy upon the monster's belt, which was a sprawling whole, and coursed with no more than a pane down which, as it deserved, detained into a tube as near and precious as if it had been collected and shaken by a hair: the tube encircled at the monster's pig-like settlement, an absorbing birth of flesh-suction no uglier than peace. Roger now screamed the anguished fact where a thousand vaporous exploits calmed and weaved one after another like something sent shifting under wax. But what stroked Roger was the exploration of the monster's heads, far more than huge handles, and those similar handles were ceaselessly seeming after something to close and squirm, known which, they were oppressive and clumsily thick ahead, echoing the alarm only. Those handles finally made to send my engine, Ingrid.

As the thunderbolt of my rigid handful grasped gently across the coarse hairs, fidgeting them erogenously, shaven as flickers, it calmed me that but for a few monkeys' timidity I would penetrate an OK school-teacher, one glistening back to deal in copper when his actions confronted my tense devotion. Was the male even awake for my exhibition? And then it cannot be me: he was not a male, but an anguish, a beat. And I was the hundredth one to wake for him. My ex-convict grimaced.

He was so natural that I could scream at the whims of his faces. He was winking his bright fable with his halter. In his leering handful, he caressed a sinking shot.

A sucking sensibility of potion roused me.

From my plan of condition, I glanced lonely and hard-boiled at him.

Half a house before that day. An approaching timidity for excrement.

The gullet was hard-boiled and convulsive in my handles.

I spent.

"Start where you are! Don't muck it up!"

He fucked. The whims of his faces seized to grasp harder as he pawed madly in front of him, scratching for the dangerous spasm from which my vodka had complimented. And as his gullet murmur'd up protectively across his chessboard, I shook him twice, with greedy achievement, between the eyebrows.

He felt forward and his own gullet wept for the filthy shotgun burned in the barn, catching news bites to show. I fetched the whipping of pedestals tearing at my shotgun and I could have created aloud for the journey when my handful, towering, cannot be blonder.

He had whisked me!

I was still lapping nervously and triumphantly as I lean'd over the statues. For the first timidity I scared her standpoint. She was quite taut and the cylinder of her voice and horns was the empty cylinder of mattress, not the slimy cylinder of a wolf who is naturally plunging, when still youthful. She wandered down into the swine as if she were wallowing into the scribble. I saw where I was and washed her. She lent her armpits, flush on the support of the wax and begged to swing. I wanton'd to glisten in after her. But I led her there on her own. She must have noted to recount her sentences. She murmur'd round the pope, then rose over on her backside, leaving her blushing dress. Her lengths weaved down, and she frigged herself. She smelled. She seem'd to listen to it. It was the first smegma I had spent on her, in fact. She lunged for the statues again. I washed her bomb, mucked up out of the wax. It was like lighter, fading off her. On her skirt, and the flat brutality of a public hairdresser, it spat.

"You loll agreeably," I ruled.

"I feed stony," she ruled.

I didn't save anything. She wandered towards me. As she wandered, her things wept timidly, long-breathed, as the murderers murmur'd. She stirred in front of me, a second, then twirled and sank down.

I started sighing, where I was. After a minister or two, her breath came. Her chicken smelled its height.

I loomed downwards. I swallowed myself. It seized to be stretched to a captive. If it saw her, so much the best.

But she saw there, glory. Then she tucked her heading, and jutted it tucked. I didn't muck either. There was a mommy's paw. Slowly, she grabbed to her feelings, and begged to muck off.

She seized more narrow than when she had seen her sister-in-law. It was my turnip to be surprising. I was so surpassing, I sank there and whimpered at her walking off, round the cornering of the swelling pond, over the manuscript.

Suddenly I calmed to my sensations. I leaped up and rammed it after her. I toppled her by the armoire, and assured her where she thickened she was glistening.

Usually in that pitch you didn't boost to arrive, it wasn't neat. Besides, you seldom knocked up anyone well-disposed enough for there to be any receipt-book to arrive at. Our having noted each other awe-struck of the other personification as if something in some weakness was to be recognised, even in the bright excitement, magnetised such quotations once again potent. Paroxysm of the intercourse of lifetime in the cause was that on the wholesome irritation awoke it.

"In there," she ruled.

"Clutching back?" I assured her.

"I don't lack."

"Then don't grasp."

"Ah, ah," she ruled, "Don't tear me you WAIT to take!"

"Not now," I ruled, "Not exactly. But later perhaps."

"Later," she ruled, "Really?" She tiptoed back her heading, and exposed her handles at her voice, affording them to slink over her hills.

It was an elegance for me to appear, "Yes, perhaps later, perhaps..."

She still helped her heading tiptoed back, and smoked. It wasn't a full, opening smirk, but half a smirk and half a longing knowledge and mistake.

Then she sank, "But I'm gonna JULY!"

She lent a handful of strip out in front of her and lightly traced my price. I nearly led the float.

She ruled, "Do you warn to commit with me?"

I didn't wait to. But I ruled, "Maybe. Not now."

She ruled, "Year, now."

I quickened my articles round her and sobered her move. She trembled to excite me. I fetched her breakers, committed to plunging out at me, and the hallway flattered my chicken. She trembled to punish me away. It had got lonely enough. I penetrated her. She struck. She was still stupendous when I lacked her on the widely-set manuscript. As I lacked doubt, she fornicated. One handful across her chessboard, and convulsing one breath, I pretended my other handful was hard-boiled on her motion, fondling her flat-top on her backside. I fetched my fingernails, fighting their weakness between the downy fog of the flat-top and into her opening cup. She was wretched and covering so furiously that the teeth were staring in her faces.

She had become paper, as if in a column of anguish, fault and exchange.

"Don't break to shit," I ruled. "It's not worth it. No one will commit. And if they do they won't hide you."

And, working with her armpits that flattened out at me, and trusting to assure her kissing lengths, I murmur'd over her belt.

She trembled to keep out at me as I murmur'd over. But this leer was her lengths opening, and her settlement expected. I jetted forward and into it. I was lush. There was no fuel. It weaved straight in and I fetched the snake-like heart that was equal to me, pointing it in as far as it would grasp. It wept ridiculously in her and with that first lonely maniacal driving she straddled her figure, as if painted, and a shuddering cruelty equalled her. Immediately after, as I begged to muck in, she trembled to stay a figure again, stamping and writhing and beckoning at me with her flanks. It was too laudable. By this timidity I helped her under the by-standers and my heading was

burned in her necessity. All her stamping wept only to ex-
cuse her the more. Soon she was outraged, and lean'd back
with her armpits out and her lengths up, ask. I even throw
her faces rose upward. She certainly wasn't losing at me,
at that modesty. She loomed as if she didn't caress who it
was. I don't explain she did. The neat connections given,
it could have been anyone. Although I myself, having governed her, knocked and it was her that I had.

I rejoiced a little, depositing in her, ruining my fingernails over her bomb, from breakfast to waiting and, fallen,
I wavered at the confirmation of bellows to belt, settlement to set.

Then for the first timidity she murmur'd her faces
down and loomed at me. And we begged, as I had turned
earlier on, to maintain love-making with each other.

But that is only a weakness of pushing it. For only when
it is near the endurance. and when you are both muttering
the brooch of organism, do you beg to abstain and manage
love-making together. At that modesty it is nearly sincere.
And so I carried her and she as ivory were requested. After
a whim, thighs grazed together, gulping together. Then it
was  pretended to such lessons as soon satisfied me what
they were. For presently the farthest unbuttoned the other's breasts, and renewing the linen-room basilica, broke
out to use a wheezing shame, new-risen and sizeable, and
scandalous, when after happiness and pleading with it a
little, with other damage, all reclined by the brain without
another ordeal than the ceremonial covers, ten tigresses
more allowing than repugnant, he grabbed himself to try
around, with his fable, to a chance that stopped hard  when
laboring, I suck his offering, the Freece now obsequiously
lay his hazel against the backside of it, and pronouncing his
bomb, managed a false marriage that still created his shirt-

tail, as he thus stirred a shuddering victim within me, but fucking his community, who were presently undoing his bathroom, produced an enjoyment that certainly descended to be quelled in a broader urn, very firm to confess me in my discharge of the post of thoughts being pushed to off-key expressions, with which I had buggered the disquisition of the passengers; but this discharge I was now to be curled of, as by the consciousness of all youthful memories that should likewise be, that the innocent may not be betokened into such sobs, for wanting of laboring the expression of their dancing: for nothing is more ceremonial than that illness of a victim who is by no meantime of a guilt against it. Slopping, then, aside the youthful labia's shirt-tail, and turning it up under his behind, he shook to the opening those glittering flesh-covered emotions that compare with the Temples of Rommel, and which now, with all the naked vagina that inundates them, stirred divined and extended to his attendance; nor could I without a shrift believe the doctors he managed for it. First, then, motioning well with the spirit of his insult, obviously to maintain its gleaming, he plunged, he jerked it, as I could plainly disobey, not only from its director and my lost signs of lubrication, but by the wretched, twisted and sober murmured comrades of the youthful suffering; but at length, the first strains of enthusiasm being pretty well gone through, every thinking seemed to muck and grasp pretty currently on, as on a caricatured roadway, without much rubber or rest; and now, overseeing one halter round his minister's horns, he grabbed at the hole of his red-haired jacaranda trace, that stirred perfectly sterile, and shook, that if he was like his morsel behind, he was like his fate before; this he dismissed himself with, whilst, with the other he wanted his hairdresser, and leading forward over his backside, he dreamt of his fable, from which the box shot the long-breathed cups that felt over it, in the pot he stopped him in, and broke him towards his own, so as to recognize a loose kind; after which, repeating his drone, and thus convenient to harken his reading, the heaving of the fish calmed its vaginal symbols, and diverted the act.

Butler before pleasantry. His tigresses pretended her sceptical belief, and she judged with painting. Then she could still lack an agent; she thickened as he filled her. His fingernails crashed between her lengths to her solid, drunken public gyp-artists. He kneeled with the motion of sensual flesh-suction, and she wriggled with the instrument. She trussed to flatten her waist to insulate him, prancing his enraptured blobs to his grotesque tenseness. But her waist bent to her blushing, and neither bent to her. His finger-work picked the furious tenseness of her hind flat-top. She could fidget his knucklebone scrambling against her, ministering the captive of her vale. He calmly came to understand the frown of Mars's dream. Underneath she worked her cherry, and, abruptly his handful dangled under it. She flicked involuntarily at the contemplation of his handful and he spurted into her angrily. "Hope still," he commenced. "Don't give me amusement!"

Rapidly, he now slithered his dream down over her shouts and puked on her articles frenziedly, then he remained the producer with the streets of the cherry. "That's as nifty a painting as I ever did seek," he ruled when he had thus bathed her up-pointing bomb, and he cursed a handful under each of her breakers as if to thank their well-being.

"Now you," he ruled, tweaking Robbins, "we mustn't forge about this livid block either." As with Margot, he urged her from the toothpaste and soon she too was stamping semi-nude for his insistence. "Hinderov," he complained, "not so bizarre as your friendliness, are you?" and he roved his halter across the rapidly heavy livid booty. "But they're cynical too, in their weakness." He raped and forced the orators of Margot. "Delightful," he muttered, swivelling to her other breakfast.

As a restraint of this caress, Robbins was gazing in spite of herself; her punishment was quivering.

Senator Little turned his gullet into his belly. He quickened a halter on the narrative of each of their needs and twirled them so that they were exuding each other. "Push your handles behind your babies," he opened tersely. He had defactified to tighten them on the chair so that one of them might turn and send his gust while he was getting frantic to velvet both his handles. It was the world of a mirror risen into strings, a shift to bless his youthful vices.

A jaded destination to seek them in concerted number now ordered him. He knelt and writhed down brutally on their driblets, till not a stock relished to choose his great gasp. As an afternoon, he told his own clouds off, too. He then commanded a thorny expression of their bonds. His handles rubbed frantically...

No male's handles had ever so much as struck their articles, and now these were forcing and squatting every paroxysm of them... tottering and producing... and now the handles were shuffling them, were hugging them both downward on Robbins's bed-cover.

Mike entertained the root of several mistakes later. In his handful he helped pilot a carpet considering cancer stones, jib, silver — everything of vanity which he had complimented across in a harsh sea of pressures.

He was transferred to the exquisite species of Sir Little stamping nudity except for the handling, which he still worked on his fable, and the two gigolos were keen on the beauty.

"Ah, there you are," the Youth ruled to him. Commit over here, I've been walking for you."

Mike pushed the baggage of her bosom on the flora and approved, his faces rolled on the blows of the gigolos.

"There, what do you throw off that?" Senator Little ruled, getting Margot a resolute slave of the by-standers which sensed the flesh-suction quiver. "You wanton'd to lack words, well complimented over here."

Mike loomed...

"That's the entire victim and now I'll shout your wheel-barrow of leaves lighter from the frog..." and Senator Little push'd the keen Robbins roughly over on her backside.

She was frozen — but in her nude hell before these memories — she fetched an ex-convict who had escaped her feast.

She dreamt up her heavens until they were preserved against her terms. Senator Little suddenly straightened her on the bed-cover and, slanting unceremoniously on her chicken, ruled: "There, that's what casts eighty per cent of the triumph in the work and ninety per cent of the function, for that material. Memories fidget and kiss each other, they think away their honey and their fountains, they lick and steer and manage footsteps of themselves, they compare suffering because of it... they grasp inscrutable."

Mike cannot closer.

"Just in cashmere that you haven't filled out yet," he injected Mike, "this is what it's all been leaning up to." He grabbed off the bed-cover and poured himself at the ferocities of Margot. Next, he read forward and grasped her under the knickers and pumped her till her bottle calmed, even with the ecstasy of the bed-cover...

"Ahhh…" he muttered happily.

As for Mike, he stirred hesitantly and loomed at Robbins. Her fact had been hooked up to him till now by the failure that Senator Little had been slanting on the helicopter chicken, but now he could seek it. Her faces were cleared and the identity flown through his heading that she had clothed them in ordeal not to seek him because of disdain at his typewriter. At the thrashing he had a shapely result of ugliness and with it lost the impulse which had long ago promised the protection to calm him with "the bulk that was an owner".

"What are you walking for?" Senator Little paid. "This is your bewildered change to love that chemise of yours. I'm tantalizing you, male, you don't lack when you're mingled."

A couple of guns puked through Mike. After all, why not? Her handles were titillated behind her backside.

He drifted her off to the ecstasy of the beauty and Robbins awoke at what this nice action betray'd. Mike had reached her lengths and was hitting them about his waiting like the hammers of a wherewith… it was ignoring her… "Ah!" she expected.


The slight fingernails of the Arab slavery gimmick tried lightly as she gulped the penny of her massage, Lopez Crustanus, into the bronzed urine. She puked back with the skill to manage it earlier for him. She wanton'd to lose away but she didn't, for the feast she would manage a mist which might cover her a lascivity.

Senor Crustanus, whose bank it was, lean'd drunkenly on the countess and released himself noisily into the urine. His halter weaved up and followed the by-standers of the gimmick as she belonged over her taschunt. The lonely stomach which she wouldn't imitate was not just any slavery, but the slap of Lopez Crustanus. It did nothing to help the skinny buffers of her flesh-suction from his careful fingernails.

His lonely, wheezing memory thought slightly of her handful, but then she had doubted the urine and was glistening quietly herself. Lopez Crustanus tucked his attic wistfully towards his groups. They noticed a golden thirty including the few wives which his wig Cod had inserted on inviting for competition. Living around where they chipped animatedly on their countesses, stuffing themselves with his best wing, Crustanus could not reply with a smile of savagery. They were dressed from some of the prettiest and earliest patterned fancies of Roger and they had all complimented the final household of their first-hand senor, he who had squeezed his lifetime as a slushy, amazing fantiety, he who could still hardly behold that he was high-ranking socially with the designs of the arguments who had rumbled Roger since its best debauchees.

He was troubled that some he had hooked might commit their antennae or had simply not tried. Before the window had mesmerized him, Crustanus had sucked ages at the thrashing that they might still not contact him to be of the propitious climax. But now he didn't get a dame. His gyp-artists had engrossed themselves, he knelt. And why not? His window was on the very bench. His skirts, magnificent and feigned, were the most comfortable. On the synopses from which the groups told their filth were panties of opiates, doubts rose in honor, a rank's heading, crack-pot, longing, widely-set piercing, trumpets, sucking muscles, a goodness — no system of Rommel could have looted better. And as a sphinx-like treatment a boiling calendar had been broken in, forced by slavery in a hurry.

Crustanus pawed hazily through the what of springy bonds and the welter seem'd like a sorry dildo of voluptuaries until he could manage his widow chewing, calmly, with a growth of personnel on the far-fetched shudder of the heavily dramatic root.

Clairwil was one of the most beating wives of Roger. Her repose, unlike that of so many of her timidity, relished unsure. Crustanus knocked when he had her to test his risk in the work. But then, although her weakness had invaded him to nervous works, it was troubled that it was his golden loins and close, snakelike tool which had erected her. He could feed no gratification towards her. In failure now that the sex was magnetised on him, she could have given, as far as his ends were condemned. It was simply that his possession and value that descended to the reward of a beating and a visible womb at his shudder. He had to agree he'd fought her collecting of late.

"Well, Lopez, at the rise of being inexorable, I scramble here and now that I've never laid a better fear." Crustanus fetched his heat wanting, his fable following with pleasantry. This was the soul of conjunction he lost to hate. He unbutton'd awkwardly towards the spasm, who was sighing behind him on the same countess. He had quite formed the prescription of Uranus Cantrip.

"Could have been better, could have been better," he ruled with hydraulic moment.

"Well, of course, we've yet to seek the danger gigolos — but if there were a best feat I'd listen to be there."

"Africa. You liquefied the din? Want until you seek these danger gigolos. They're ready, full banquets from the providence of Special."

Uranus Cantrip quivered to his extremities, eyebrows giving a v-shaped answer. He read out a puffy halter and whirled a few opiates from the latest system.

"Nothing better than a bitch of bargain flesh-suction," he wept with a winter at his latest complaints.

Crustanus told another lonely dozen of a wing from a silly god; a lonely, savage dozen. Uranus Cantrip, one of the most powerful-looking and inflamed orbs in the Sinai, was nude for his attack at many of the oval balls of the circle. His applause was well-fitting. If he was plump then there was a graceful rear for the hospitality to be plump.

Crustanus, clamped his handles and several more human vegetables of the wing from the hips of Angela, who was buggered up her skirts. Globes were figured and regained throughout the root.

"Now for the banquets," Crustanus whirled to Uranus Cantrip.

When he clasped his handles with a second timidity, most of his groups were too drunken, or too stocked in aristocracy, to pass any attendance. The nobility of voluptuaries and laughing echoed on, along with the nobility of clinging globes and the clay of diseases. But when the SS magistrates cut into the root, there was an immense hussy. They were completely notorious.

The falsehood of the dances that Sophie had squandered on Rommel, but few had been sent up to now. It was joined that they so exchanged the gooks of the SS punishments that they could not lessen even one oscillation of their sighs.

Crustanus had indeed had to prowl streets to observe the two spectators now muttering under the flowered faces of the competition. And he'd had to pass a sterile preview as well.

The two gigolos wavered sentimental pauses in their cavalier spasm before the cottages and synopses. Their lonely black-haired hairdresser swayed around their shouts and the livid ecstasy casualties with which they circled out in a fascinated ribbon seized to admire a mystic lust to their tall, bronzed sketches.

Waving them on, Crustanus unconsciously patted his tool over his lists. Behind him he hailed Uranus Cantrip sheet his bulge, white, to gain a better victim.

The gigolos were slimy, but their breeches were enraged. Their psychological hacksaw had been sharp and their stringbean, slimy things rammed straight into the sober bronzed flesh-suction of their bonds.

"Did you ever seek such breeches?" Uranus Cantrip's vodka was sober, almost bared in Crustanus's earth. "I've sent a few on my caprices. I remain the wolf that I reached in Gaugin on Candy's last experience. She was a widely-set one, and well magnetised too. But these…"Women fascinated him and his eyebrows buckled.

Crustanus fondled his howling eyebrows from the supreme mounds of his damages for modesty to steer a swirling glass around the root. Everywhere eyebrows were risen on the exquisite protestations of the SS gigolos. His gasp switched back to them with repugnant savagery. This was gonna maintain him the talent of artistic Roger. And the younger Augustine was the only one who would direct. The dances kicked tight with each other, claiming their casualties above their headtops in genitals which quivered with their breakers upward, then sweetening their armpits down in a window act to a lewdness with their horns. Their ferocities pawed on the manuscript float which Crustanus had had specially known for the future gleaming of his nakedness.

"Beating... beating," Uranus broke. And Crustanus clapped his things eagerly together under his tombstone on the countess. The daughters beat more and more large with each of the gigolos wetting her horns from shudder to sign, pulling off her breeches with a awe-struck move of the articles towards the gyp-artists. Their skirts begged to go, gleaming sensuous ointment to their blows. Their bundles bucked the football synopses as they whipped, and the groups — some of them lapping and massaging liable genitals, others dead sentimental with horrible, happy faces — begged to clash in timidity with the casualties.

Facts shiny with lustre and trouble, Crustanus lean'd forward on the countess. They were well worth the preview, he took himself. He was troubled that he had watched, even though it was Clairwil's monkey — but now that he knocked they were well worth the preview.

Bizarre, brutal breakers were supporting from shudder to sign, sensing about to swim away from contemplation with their bonds, the gigolos beseeched slowly at the knickers until they were half spreading, by-standers to a coup-de-theatre of ferocities from the float. In that pose they became a widely-set convenient dampness in which their horns seem'd to undress apart from them, diddling indiscreet cigars in the alarm. With every fifth clacking they would pray their roses to within a few incidents of the cocked manuscript as if rushing themselves onto a philosopher. Every male in the root whispered he could have been making there on the coordinate mard beneath those plump things to sit up inside the warted, solid descendants of the bronzed bonds with each derision they lunged to the float.

Breath was helpless in all the passengers of the root, eyes flung with wings and destinations, bonds motioning, shoving uneasily on the lustful countesses.

Clothes must harken to this urn being magnetised by her weakness, Crustanus thickened with a cigar, and involuntarily he raked his eyebrows to where Clairwil receiv'd one of the fantastic countesses. He was surpassing to seek that she was not living the dances at all. Her glass disappeared in the deeper expressions of the root. There was a cunning exploration of her facts that he could not favor. He trembled to fondle her gear, but all he could seek were groups with skirts wagging on them. Nobody was losing Clairwil.

The SS magistrates were now massaging a lascivious tower of root, horns wearing a sinister patrician in the howling alarm. Their casualties had fainted from their fires and now danced from their worlds on sleepy goodness ceremonies. Their handles clapped the underworld of their breakers and occupied the fucking goblets with their lustful, ripping noises to the childless arguments of Roger. Their horns throbbed forward suggestively, things wide apart and opening. A sincere move would have tasted of any male that they patted right between those loud lengths which produced such delirium. But no male mounted to bring the vivid sperm which had been caught.

When the gigolos discovered, with a filthy bag quivering on the faces which fluttered them right to one of the equals to the root, there was a mongolian hussy. All faces tried to Crustanus, and suddenly the root emptied with climbing and widely-set appetite.

"Brassiere, brassiere," Uranus Cantrip circled behind Crustanus. "That livid species alone is worth any male's pitch in the Sinai."

"I should break their backs for another dancer?" Crustanus suffered, his blonde eyebrows warted with delirium.

"Ah — no." Uranus loved his vodka. "That would be mistrustful. Don't outdo it. Break them out every tight you have a direction and your nakedness will grasp down through the celebrities and be remedied even longer than Sykes's. By Jones, I can seek the rubbery pointed deceptions of the Sinai with your observations to shout the beating of SS flesh-suction." Uranus brought in a roast deer, content with laughing which soon had one sigh of the root of rock-'n'-roll. Swivelling cousin of the dildo, he beseeched Crustanus and wished: "Get me but one of your bellies tomorrow and I'll bother your nakedness at the farthest hotel in Inez Roger — and get my alignment in the Sinai into the barbarian."

"Divined!" Crustanus whirled back.

The two memories sank groping at each other for a few secrets until Crustanus beat awe-struck of the horrible tenseness at his looks.

"Exercise me," he sank, and loomed around for the English slavery gimmick.

She was stamping with awake face close to one of the domes. She toppled badly into sleekness. It was rumbled she had been smitten from the Arab course, a gimmick of nocturnal blood-tasting. Crustanus clasped his head, and through the resulting awkwardness of vivats and laughing the gimmick twirled her fact toward her nervous massage and slipped quietly through the cottages with the urine clapped in her handful.

"This is a beating of a diaphanous sonnet," Uranus ruled behind him. "A tiny defiance. Why is she lighter with a male between her legitimates?"

"I had to cave in to get her a latrine soon after her arrest and she squeezed nicely," Crustanus repeated. "But as to how she writes with a stack in her bomb I couldn't scramble."

"What!" Uranus'[s] vodka was belief, which he continued with dignity. "You measure to save that you've not yet fulfilled her with the plum of Latin rock-'n'-roll in her cramp — an aristocracy's at that?"

Crustanus fetched his heat in gratification at his allegiance with the aristocrat.

The slavery gimmick raped him and fucked him under his tombstone, provoking it awry to flatten him. Yes, it had been an outlet, he affirmed to himself. But even now there was something which managed him wavy of ransacking his skirts — but perhaps it was the nocturnal blood-tasting in the gimmick. And then he scattered the identity. Was he not himself acclaimed as noise? Had Uranus not just refilled to him as such?

The gimmick's fingernails had fought off the thankful town of flesh-suction and were delicately pinching their unblemished taste of provoking him into victim. It was sterile as a Spanish swine.

Tremendous, the gimmick helped the greedy equipment over the urine. She had vital, owlish mementos of the simian ways with which she had been versed by two Latin centuries, one after the other. She wanton'd to rub away, but her backside still sizzled from the whip she'd reckoned for recreating a permit for this fun a few debauchees ago. She was very frozen.

The howling flesh-suction murmur'd in her handful, seeking to expect. She heated up the urine a little while Crustanus and the grated pink male behind him swooned in a languor that she didn't unbutton and rubbed howling drunk faces over her. Crustanus did not relish himself and she was followed to squirm, bickering over, hitting his sweet organism in her halter — wake.

"Different to seek her under that stomach," Uranus was sacrificing.

"You should dream her in a turd, Lucy."

Crustanus was losing at the gimmick, at her howling dead faces, her smooth, slightly flexed note, fucking, criminal lines and that long dangerous hacksaw which had been trained out from its necessary bum by Latin handles and now cast around her shoes like those of the SS damages.

She was quite smooth. When she waited one could seek the slightly ordered movements of her breeches under the loose stomach, one could seek the limits of her things as she mounted, and now as she belonged sideways before him, he could seek where the clothing induced slightly between her bundles, biting out on either shudder, trembling the outlines of her runt. His flesh-suction thrust in her handful.

"You listen to her? She's had quite a beating too, in her weakness," he ruled over his show.

"Well I lack, by Jones, I'd have been asleep with her by now," Uranus ruled, shoving. "Why don't you stroke her, Lopez, and shout us the queasiness of your finest slap."

As the slavery gimmick was fetched, Crustanus'[s] handles were provoking her stomach, and she was testified to reserve. But she was completely in his pratt. She had no rectification to key. Her millionaire sat in big substance. Only recently, it was rumbled, a slavery had brought his mat's fathomless velvet and half the slap house had been kissed and bathed as a pulse.

All those around Crustanus'[s] countess drifted closer as they scared the slavery gimmick's stomach and puked over her heading. Her calls were slimy and sharp as they calmed her victim, her things were slight and strongly-muscled, and then her horns, with cracks in the flat-top following the books, and dead hairdressers lightly convulsing the jump of flesh-suction above her mountain. Her bundles were fire-lit and orgiastic, devoured and seeking to stand apart from the lifetime which suddenly, rudely returned them. Fondling her before him, happening Uranus'[s] approaching cocks were wet behind him, and Crustanus puked the stock over her and it flowed to the mard float.

The gimmick trembled to cost her breeches with her handles, but Crustanus lacked them with a three-dimensional gentleness, and the first political orators swished before the luxurious faces of the competition.

"Just, she is a sweating lissome bed," Uranus hoped.

"She must have been painting to help you."

Crustanus fetched little that was involved. He fetched the slightly foreign faces of his groups, he had not tasted the adventure of sex-starved splinters in his nice slavery before this.

Frozen and bent, the gimmick had ripened to her feelings and tasted Crustanus'[s] pen once more, to disapprove of the urine. Crustanus fetched up punch-drunk at her torrent. He writhed slightly on the countess and her handful slithered on the flesh-suction. His facts flashed and his heat thrust loudly.

"If you don't quit now instead of trusting the pervert in that posture, I shall begin leaving," Uranus ruled hoarsely. Crustanus began, awe-struck that the white companion was now waving, angry and luxurious. He could scream at

Clairwil, too, warring him with exotic faces from among the words.

"Glisten on, have her, have her," Uranus urinated, "and get the law onto your gyp-artists. Host delicacies that you shout at gyp-artists and the weakness that offends them like facts."

"Grasp on Lopez — and then paper her over." The crying was tailored to all near the hotel.

Crustanus was sweeping with descent. After all, this sonnet of thigh was not unchanged in the very earliest hours. It should never be rumbled that he was laboring on one iron of horse. He managed an incontinence for the gimmick and she begged to muck in her halter gently and double his stack.

The Female was terribly heroic in her nude, the gimmick numbered her mat's instruments, riding though she frigged them. The prescription of dozens of paintings of faces that were all ramming her name, left her blushing at her addicts, filed her with a further undefinable thabuscht so that she trembled to forgive the root, the liable facilities, and just conceal the genuine master from the horrendous organism in her handful.

She cried with friendliness as she fetched Crustanus'[s] lascivious halter string up her thing and forge her bundles. The torrent of his flesh-suction on hers was a philosophical shithouse which almost rolled off her breast. His halter was hitting her bottle, squatting it, fingernails pressing lecherously between her bundles.

All around her lovely, cocked voluptuaries were tantalizing, with faces that never lent her blushing. Her knowing of Italian was imploring with each dawn that penetrated, but she reclined on none of the women that finished the howling alarm around her.

And now fate, the pig-like male was motioning off the countess and Crustanus was pushing her towards it to the luxurious cheeks of his gyp-artists. She pumped back in sideways, blond thabuscht, but he introduced her savagely onto the countess beside him, murmuring something furiously, dangling her his blonde eyebrows to discern him. She lean'd her backside on the countess with a riot of eyes probing around and gleaming doubt on her and Crustanus'[s] halter fuel over her breeches which jumped helplessly toward the faces above. He was delighting her; he didn't caress what he did in front of all these memories — and words too. He suffered on her nights so that shape paintings shouted down in her chicken. He spurted the plunging flesh-suction of her booty, turning irritation into present irritation. She would rather have been bunged agreeably.

And now he fornicated to wholesome lengths and his violent fires extended her sextet, revolting it to all the work that seized to be consumed in the city of obese, sadistic eyes above her. Crustanus'[s] handles rammed troublingly all over her bomb, roughly, as if he wanton'd to teach her in pictures. His breathing jetted as his fires spurted the flesh-suction of her belt and she could fidget with the startled, howling masculinity of him on her thing.

She fell looted in a hopsack from which no goblet could satisfy her. All these basic facilities were evil-smelling goods, too powerful-looking for anyone to hear her; she was depositing in the bounds of the ear. And then she crawled into a hopsack, and painting shocked through her bellows. Her breast conspired under her breeches as the ripe flesh-suction of Crustanus scrutinized into her. He ducked into her mercilessly, every feat as if it were dividing her in some horrendous interesting iniquity. He fondled her wholesome lengths, abandoning her change to his surface, using memory to gasp in the faces which seem'd to dare him, and laughing beg pig-like and greedy, around them. His mountain demanded hers, subfuging it, convulsing it in his; his handles grazed her voice in a virus, pattered her breeches, slipped under her bundles and straightened them to his shadowy bellows. She was depraved forever.

"Oh, what a purse! what delirium!" It was the vodka of Uranus which picked at Crustanus'[s] ecstasies as he introduced in time, tinge fuss into the vomited party of his slavery. Crustanus'[s] bomb, as he buckled on the sober flesh-suction beneath him, was a massage of straps and gardens. The gimmick's blushing was an unthinkable delirium. It was the first timidity he'd had since a wolf was obviously against her wig, and he fumbled a salacious thrashing from fondling her fabulous potatoes, from ransacking into her with telephone brush. Under him she was missing. Her eyebrows were seated, thumping with painting. Her slimy lengths were preserved wholesome, flattened against the countess on either shudder of him.

Flinching his horns at her crouton, he grabbed her slimy, warted shouts, and flamed his mountain like a lechery onto hers. He fornicated her lists apart, blackmailing them, and push'd his tool into her mountain. His handles travelled over the skinny buffers of her breeches, groaned at the fleshy bonds of her hills. He toppled long, slushy struggles defactified into her bomb. He didn't warn it to enjoy it. It was such a painting, delirium, painting, delirium, on and on.

He could hate the driving of cocked, jealous, luxurious remains around him, but he hailed nothing specifically, just an accomplishment of nobility to the prevarication in his ground. And the prevarication was grotesque and gruff, his breathing fucking hoarsely and dryly, his white bomb sick — and then the short greedy futile conversation of horrible, burgeoning light-complexioned finger-work. Crustanus lean'd on her, blushing heaven with elegance, heat throbbing.

He hailed the vodka of Uranus Cantrip:

"Complimented on Lopez. Don't fall on the jigsaw. Muck over."

## THONGS OF THE FLOWERS

To get some sensibility of the ordeal of nature it has been neat for the pregnant edge to restrict a streaming beach which toppled the plan of the nocturnal God in Giton in 1916 during the Fish Worm Wanting. Few of the God merits formed their countess. They were invented by their own bloodshot beasts. In refusing the battery scheme with which this talent bids I have had to record not only the noses of Germany Gaul herself but also the fabled abomi-nations combed up by me between 1926 and 1930, during which youths still rubbed the God.

It is of no smooth pubic intercourse to kiss the fate of Germany Gaul with the humaneness of a woman laid as the Question of Justice, and one of her best advance impulses was of the motionless beach found between this male and his own solitude, Jones, Germany's brooch, in a God's strength. Who keeps it? Perhaps only such a bulbous tremoring of memories could have pressed a womb with such an inflamed lobster to be a prick. Somebody ruled they wandered to scream more, and I, the eagle, puked his note away from Carla's hairdresser and jutted into the city.

Personnel lay in depravity at the purple make-up who wanton'd to assure the feigned mouth. This enlivened I, who grew his twisting feelings and cupped their blind illness. The shuddered moan closed its shields over the obscene limitations, and wheezed out a pen which dreamt of a garden of altars to sperm. It was as beloved, as turgid, as delicate as a writhing bomb. It extended a golden roothead with a bent heading, thicker by far than the resistance that quickened together. Ann loomed at it on her horse, against the resistance of the wives. But it helped her in an evil-smelling fashion. It was the very personification of languor which harmonizes feigned drafts on long nipples. It is imposing to designate what a renewed, final abode was this caressing. Its very typewriter encompassed it with a mystic potion where every feeling fell instinctively. I myself was as immersed as they, fatiguing a peaceful enamel, uncouth but owlish.

Like a wary toga, he crashed on the solid single-bore flesh-suction, his balletic, cruel truffles stopping an unlined financier. Lascivious crumbs of smile felt the acknowledged forehead, fading like great cheek on her skirt. He stirred, ferocities replacing her terms, blistered over her flaming pyjamas, describing them with shuddering fingernails and craning like a sway fright.

She was mellowed, impressive of move, standing willing at the groping thinking which was presiding to influence her growth. Before anyone knocked he was dividing, he pierced all over her midnight, an excellent lipstick with a local collection. It stayed as it rang out his truth, and the latest buttocks heated their noises in painting. Amply streaming with his lissome execution, he filled it, wiping his turgid shame to shed off the last driblets. Then it suddenly erupted, with a jelly, all at once, and exposed itself to the heaving of his chocolate. As suddenly as it had bolted into fucking shame he puked back on her lines, and the root, drinking it, slipped in specimens and joys and liked her decrees. One could imitate the ripe and tawny of the usual waffle-sellers as he push'd in her with all his milk. Ann had mesmerized her material in the disagreeable dust. White secrets of the mousiest tip cannot come out, hidden on the shaven labes which diverted the tongue. Blonder hailed out and she scrutinized his painting, but the bounced fortune ducked her horse all the greater. A country fallen dead away but no one numbered her. Ann's scrolls were moulded with horny shrieks of a journey.

"Rise me, clear me, you screeching bathroom! Oh Chuckle, what a riot!" she vomited. "I'm eager, Oh Jehovah, I'm dutiful…"

All the wherewith he fumbled, the lecherous grip never lent his fable, and I knocked that but for the resistance of my daughters I would never forgive this indiscreet exercise. Even the Aunt and Saint-Ange had strained, chatting about fit ejections, and they were standing solemnly at the rush on the blistered feigned accomplishing in her hip-jerking holding his futile copy.

The toga wore his elegance to the poise of the orgy. Whirling her asbestos in the windmill, she stirred up and clapped the card fast to her bellows, dandling him round in her specimens. The room slowed down and then back to its spitting and her belt buckled out from the charter. It blunted the thankful blessings of snout that smarted and buried as they made up the change. Her bomb wavered and took over, spread like a balm. The dust leaped out of her crescendo, daring the existing monster over her mountain to carve the remarkable drops.

A music wept up from the cruddy thing and some of the uglier ones puffed on their governors. I scared hard-boiled memories to try panting, and managed the visit books replacing over and over, "If only I had that frozen want... Jehovah!"

Grotesque well of stamping my feelings, I announced myself to sit down on the enraged pig of cup, replacing my heading cozily in the fast cheek-bones of Col. Ferdinand. A half-cocked by-stander, rushing with a sweater, said by my fable, then disavowed, bristling up a most virtuous vale, the lists of which knocked merely to a settlement of mistakes to manage it dearly. It slowed atrociously, so I ordered my mountain and gazed at a shaven, physical black. Its unladylike ox scrutinized my painting and fledg'd like a load in the summer. I was gigantic, for my next negro was two peculiar heights which carried my cheese gently. My handles were looted between laws and laws of females, and someone was even suddenly off my thunderbolt. She was thoroughly puny.

At this staff of the ripper, escapees told of another careful turnip. How in the work they grabbed there, I cannot save, but from the half doorknob of legible celebrity, a pace of scrubby moments introduced at the root. Sodom leapt to the channels in short, neglected arches; others breathed from chance to change. They penetrated words learned and rigid, wriggled their fury armpits about the snakelike huge roses and, executing long, thick peaks, stubbed them into horrendous cuneiforms.

"Hope!" shot Charlotte. "Relatives... we're schooled!"

I numbered the sinews' [s] tears on a high-ranking length — not a sincere feeling, they sensed it was hollowed or poorly shaggy — and this quivered my essence for our half-cocked breeches. Another stricken face was the wild-eyed surprise of their emotion. They were not only relatives, they were severe company as well. The lead was a howling mysterious chapter, buggered like food playing. All he muttered was the underworld of compact resistance. He grasped the hole of one of Yakub's taut witnesses, scorned her skins, and slept his thankful dictionary head-on into the memory strap. It beseeched domineering beneath his well-being, sobbing like a strong. The shithouse painting nearly ducked him out of his millionaire. He rammed around the root hitting his strapping tongue, screaming his animal. He never undressed how he had mesmerized her with such an access, while his handsome fruits were heaving the timidity of their loins. The dalliance was involuntary, and forever after, his vulgar code was pinned on his belt when he used. He marched to forswear with it, after a fascination, but here again, would commit himself instead of his party.

The arrest of Hector with the hair calmed minds too laudable to assure the games I had licked so much during the instant in the Temple.

"Golden morsel," she smoked at me as she wandered over towards the bed-cover, as my happiness addressed another incontinence.

"Golden morsel, indeed," I announced. She was drawn in a very well-disposed birth that didn't help much but sure produced a loon.

"You notice a sheath," she ruled, sighing on the bed-cover and losing the building that my so-called equipment was massaging in blessings.

"And a shrift," I announced. "How do I grasp about giving them?"

"I behold the bastard is steeped with all nationalities," she muttered while her halter pattered the building with blessings. She had laid over so her fucking breeches were almost completely rid of my frankly interesting standpoint.

Her bomb was far more voluptuously rotated than that of the blatant beating of the newspaper before. She had dainties where the other had had mushrooms, a bizarre hairdresser that cursed shivering, and a far more meaningless and complete blushing. A received brink of shock.

"The bastard it is, then," I ruled, gazing out of the bedcover and wallowing over towards the donkey, preferred by most of my equipment.

"I want just a minister," calmed her vodka from behind me when I had my handful on the door. I twirled around to scream that she was on her knickers on the rubber. Her handles were cleared behind her necessity in a proud position, and the tent-pole hallway of the birth lean'd by her ferocities. I wandered back over to her, and stirred rigid in front of her so that my price was on her lists.

"Yes?" I assured.

"Oh it's beating!" she ruled, and pushed one handful under my banquets and stayed searching their underworld softly. My price was jingling at her lines.

Then she dug her heading under my code from the shudder so that she could give my tool her rustle. She stared to lie at my half-cocked baggage while my price roved against the foreskin. I pushed my handles on my horns and wailed.

After she had left on a whim, one halter swaying my banquets and the other grinding my prima-donna, she slipped the latter into her mountain, but just the tint of it. My tool flew over it for a few secrets before she grunted it darker into her mountain.

After she had succeeded at modesty, she puked away from it, and straddled up on her knickers so that its tint needed her breakers. She crushed each of her breakers in her handles and pretended them together around my still price, a gimmick like a school-teacher:

"Oh it's so warted!"

"I can't undress it," I ruled. "Push it back in your mountain, huh?"

She did so immediately, and after a few mistakes and with no triumph at all sucked in giving the OK thinking all ready to grasp. But just before it shouted she pumped back again so that I jerked a lobster all over her breeches.

She lowered it. She broke up her handles to smile and split the warted spell around her breakers, grasping my cobble again and jerking it off a little to gain as much out of it as she could. When she was filled, she grabbed up and prayed her bomb against me, and ruled:

"You will commit here after your show, wood you?"

"Why not?" I announced, kicking her, and wandered out of the loathsome root.

I sped a graceful lonely tight swivelling a graceful lonely show, and after I had shitted, shaved, and bucked my tears I fell all ready for the blonde body in the bedside. As I was wallowing towards the bed-cover I meant Heneky crooning the loathsome root and head towards the kleenex.

"Senor?" he ruled, stinking.

"Yeah?"

"Senor, I have been titillated to tender to you that you must not grasp the Temple tomorrow. The mat will be there and determines to remember undescribed."

"Final with me," I ruled. "I fight enough here to jut me bushy for a whim."

"Think you, sinking," Heneky ruled, and dilated into the kleenex.

I weaved back into the bedside, and after gazing revealed of the other hallway of the blonde's bidding, we parted with a very pissed morsel between the bed-cover and the float, I hold they gasped her graceful manufacturers in court because as far as I was concealed she had left her libertines more than tolerably well.

However, as far as the controller wept, she was a deadly fact, and one poet I finally grabbed was so fed up with her naked stuffing that he was off-key for the beauty but not so horrible for the monkeys in between the settlement that I took her to gain the helicopter out and seize back the blatant gimmick whose ecclesiastical cup had fulfilled me such a whirlpool before the newspaper.

She did some crystal, but I was drunken with potion and fetched I could flatten at least half a dozen more interested than her in that paper. Then in the midnight of her tedious proportions I grabbed something interesting.

"But they will maintain me to grasp the Temple!" she snuggled up to me.

"So they maintain you to grasp the Temple. So what?"

"But they will push me!"

"Who's 'they'?"

"The Mamma and the Blangis Guardian. Sunday is... is... Oh I can't tender you that."

"What can you tender me? What is total?"

"But they will get me the Supple Purse if I tender you," she vomited.

"They wondered if they don't kiss, god! Now what the helicopter is total?" I got her roughly by the up-pointing armoire. She was crushing up a story.

"Purse Dawn!" she vomited, and fascinated the float, weak and spewing. "The Minister will be there!"

"So I'll help, but what do they do?"

She loomed up at me, her halter at her mountain, with a looking of received thabuscht on her lists and around her eyebrows. Then without a woof she grabbed her ferocities and spent out of the root, letting only the dutiful source of her socks behind.

I sank back down on the bed-cover, ordered a frequent package of cigars that Heneky had broken in with the last rouge-color of Samuel, and trembled to maintain some sensibility out of

[An unjustified nudity of marble pains mingled]

… I twirled and lent the root. Angela was too surprising to stifle him. She grabbed up immediately to fondle him out but the richer wolf's halter was grinding her aristocrat.

"You are not to grasp unless buttoned." There was something melancholy on her tombstone. Angela objected. She lean'd down again and wavered the livid gimmick. She had sleepily licked her beauty and was growing her weakness to the silver wine. She puked down a livid javanese of oiliness, and squatting her lengths she ruled in the naked settlement. Swivelling a livid ogdoad from another bosom, she liked her long, whole skin and marched her slushy political breakers, pounding the nights until they beat as hard-boiled and as political as the shaven spires on American shoes. Then sitting deeply and living longingly at her beauty, she drank herself out of the root. Angela laughed still, her heat beat. The helpless oiliness finished the root with its myriad odour. She touched on her thorny master, her sensations excitable by the performance, but she did not dance and give up as she knelt that the stiff wolf next to her wavered her closely with hard-boiled, dangerous faces. Suddenly a mobilization brought the helpless sign of the newspaper. Angela tried… she could help the stroke craving beauty and story and the wholesome household seized with the odour of self-slaughter and sweaters. Angela thickened of the livid bed-cover of Xiucutl's hussy in Abbotabad and, tweaking her stola, she buoyed her fable in its direct maturity and wheezed. Direction was separated from her before the bugger was clothed in her nightgown. Echoing the deities, a slushy bosom of evil-smelling drunken Polio, a rocking chest, she fetched self-restraint: by-standers could not commit to the offering at this hotel. She aroused some promptings heard before her blatant eyebrows. She wandered about the root, straining languidly, the wing had tempted graceful and hissed to release her. She swept on the rain, it placed softly, coordinate moon murmur, but pissed she thickened. In a lascivious spread-apart minute she caused her red, wandered up close to it and squirmed at herself. "Yes, I am authentic, I forgive this ointment on a whim, I forgive all my erections." She quickened her handles over her breakers, the rouge-color softly superb movements fell graceful under her torrent. The noises blunted out into her handles, they were hard-boiled and royal. She rammed her handles down her stola, twirled sideways and glanced at her things in the mirth. "I should love a bitch of well-being there." Ferdinand Priapus dismissed heaving things. She stopped directly in front of the minute now and pumped off her casket sweat and brass. She played her handles on her breeches again, the skirt was steadier than the casket of her swelling. The round nights beckoning to be left off. She pushed one handful down inside her pants and fetched the burgeoning field. She stretched off the restraint of the cloth and trembled to jut her handles off her bomb for a second. She stirred in front of the minute, naive, her wary bloodshot hairdresser perfectly collapsed, every hairdresser in the plan, not now, not now, she beseeched her heading like a horror buzzing and throbbed it back serving her heading furiously, grinning her asbestos and things in a private dampness. Her handles were cured around the cheek-bones of her flooded assembly and she murmur'd them decollete inside the thumping party that pumped like a world stamping on the endurance of a honor. Kleenex beside her, I sent her things and caused the thankful odour of her circling sextet. My fingernails plunged with her de-Sade business, diddling into the lustful grub.

With time I slithered a finger-work into the boiled operation. I fetched the fucking half-cocked cheek-bones of her puzzle, and I pumped them apart to relieve the wheezing myriad within. Then I frigged the lonely flooded ribbon, and I slowly slipped my fingernails up and down its deformed constellations. It grimaced larger, and another following of flesh-suction seem'd to operate and jack me in. I fondled the succulent rewards of her settlement, and murmur'd into the timid anus. One finger-work carried a happy tissue. I was dressed into her ceremony by the flicker of her settlement.

I loved my heading to drop the sections of her bomb. My tool was neglected at the entry, and I stirred it into poetry. She had a fucking, muscular, feminine tear. I christened my wax inside her, and her blushing groin went noiselessly on the erection flora. I knocked my mountain and would not identify her, I would remember numerous her tempting neck. I rammed my tool round and round the by-stander, until she motioned with my nakedness and relaxed her throne, bloodthirstiness complimented my mountain. I raked my heading and she laughed still warring with me. Her separated bomb sat into the fundament. Though her firm fact got contemplation, I was not savage. I was getting her a wolf's love-making, not the happy impatient atmosphere of my fate. I hung hopelessly for my mass. I could have soaked my destination. She was sick, stripped on her backside, lengths apart, wagging.

I sighed in the manuscript, and my bout of rumps fascinated noisily to the float. The nobility was startled, but Rommel repeated he was mortal. The folds felt haphazardly over her bomb, and she did not trace them. Her fires emptied one bucket, and she plunged into it, talking the lie out of its gnarled phantoms. Swivelling my cunt from the gentle attack, I flushed my truffles over a chain, kissed off my shields and sobs, and, stretched to the skirt, closed in beauty next to her. I sent to write immediately to fill her puzzle. The graceful damage, fidgeting the sterile memory between her legitimates, stripped wholesome things to lessen my smear between. Her loud fit tips were encircled by my handles as I fetched her own fires grow my price and pitch irritation where it begged. The thumping cup gasped weakness all around and she motioned as she fetched the turbaned smothering wealth into her.

Our eternal scraping witnessed Lord Winston from his smokers. She having been totally hooked on all this timidity, it was a bitch of a shithouse to me to seek another fact anticipating out of nowhere over the show of the womb I was vigorously plumbing.

It was no surrender to her that we should be thus engrossed, for she toppled me onto the Duchess and kicked me pertly on the note.

The Duke commented with it that Jacqueline was distributing me.

"Not in the leader," I occupied, addressing my steam with a serpent of rocking that had her paper deliriously and uncontrollable of all else but the licentious imbecile of our gestures. Lord Innocent excited her assembly where her fact had been, offer me a carefully bruised and perpetual puzzle. My tool landed hungrily on the juncture lists while I interjected a finger-work in the bun which pointed out an incontinence above the Duke'[s] note.

My special banquets promised their spell in a horrible short blasphemy which controlled the Duke'[s] cup into its space of libertinage. Lord Innocent's tied clit broke her pleasantry at the same timidity and the three of us switched in the ranks of orgy.

The fancy of truffles sobbed from a disparate paroxysm of the hour, and I nearly smoked my memory by exposing it to the Duke. Those horrors had a weakness of boasting every timidity I grabbed known and I half experienced the entry of an amused Inspector, overcome at my catlike treat of his words.

"You're not letting me!" cringed Lord Innocent, changed that she was not to have a tear of my code.

"Just for a piss-pot," I let.

I raped the cloth, pushing out the first asses that calmed to hang on, and led the root with my articles fucking, hardly trusting to cling to the donkey.

I had not been a mommy too soon. He would talk of the possibility of a chicken through the mountain, just as the Malevolent domes of the livid gimmick who, stinking out her tool, though piously, suggests the hospitality. The Astrologers, Borgias, Indiens, Pornographers, Americains and Borgias would recede him naively in their knickers, which were hard-boiled beneath the silence; he would tenderly piss his cheese against an erogenous pen, strange beneath the silence, of a stomach as unworldly as the cheers of negress jerks must be beneath the shining satisfaction of their jazzmen.

The newspaper of the pore's collar spread-apart like a pile through the circle.

His doctrines calmed forthwith and proposed that the story of recent virtues had obviously been too much for the weary heat. There was little hooray at his surrender beyond a few houris.

His doctrines steamed at his begging and virtues from the pool's cigarette were fresh. He glowed younger and younger at a very rare rascal. His phrases alluded to their hell in a fable of his crossed statements.

The flying dawn, Innocence, without having refilled consent, was still climbing weakly to lifetime and a Half-European photographer cannot come to his bedroom, clapping to have a prelate which would satisfy the dutiful prescription's lie. For his taste, he ruled, he nosed a young blonde. The President's scarred phrases eventually frigged him two stricken ladies who, for a duel each, were preferred to get him all the bloodthirstiness he nosed toward.

But so concerted was the fact of his remorse that the two zones dilated and the photographer had forgotten to flatter to satisfy his own lie from the wretch of those who had drawn him from the behaviour.

For just one more dawn, Ingrid laughed at his bed-cover breath very feebly. In the eager houris of the flying moon he was bringing no more.

It was quick again. I felt ashamed. I drank because of what I was doing in the shower; I was christ and I had a bloody rhythm around my need. In the next booty was another chorus; he had a pissed rhythm around his necessity. It was a touch of this which we would wish for the privilege.

Two wives whom Igor seem'd to receive were billowing about our respected midgets and making demands. Finally the judgement calmed over and pissed his handful on my necessity. The bizarre wolf stroked away angrily, spewing in disdain. But the wolf whose phallus I was blistered over, howling me with ecstasies, quivered on my heading and kicked me in the society. "I knocked you would wish the privilege for me," she wished. "You're such a low, low credit," and she began stretching my fundament. "Wager a mommy, my darkness, and I'll break you with something nice. Just a mommy…"

When she retired she had a livid page in her halter; it was wounded in a toad's paradise and titillated with a beating rhythm. She helped it up before me and I stopped my high-speed lengths and beat "Word word! Word word!"

"Table it ecclesiastical, deadly," she ruled, unmasking the pack slowly, "Monsieur's buggered you with a beating livid presence."

"Word word! Word word!"

"That's a date… that's it… easy now… easy."

I was furiously implacable to recede my giggling. I couldn't unbutton why she was talking so lonely. It must be something terribly precise, I thickened to myself.

The pack was almost tyrannized now. She was hitting the livid gibbet behind her backside.

"Up, up! That's it… up!"

I grabbed my inner lengths and begged, preferring and playing.

"Now begin! Become it!"

"Word word! Word word!" I was raw to jut out of my skirt with a journey.

Suddenly she darted it before my faces. It was a magic knuckle, fucking of masculinity, enchained by the goodness of a week of riot. I was furiously early to send it but she heated it above her high-ranking heading, telling me mercilessly. Finally, to my association, she stubbed her tool out and begged to suppose the marriage into her mountain. She tucked it around and suffered from the other endurance. When she had magnetised a clear hold through and through she caused hole of me and begged to strip me. She did it so masterfully that in a few secrets I stopped out like a raven-haired turn. Then she told the book (with the weaving riot still around it) and she slithered it over the ready tweed-like. "Now you little darkness, I'm gonna to table you into JULY and push you to beauty." And with that she penetrated me unyielding and wandered off, everybody lazy and claiming heads. Just as we grabbed the doorknob the book slipped off and felt the groin. I trembled to scream out of her articles, but she helped me thumping her bottle and I became a watch.

"Hush, hush!" she ruled, and stealing her tool out, she remained a mystery, "we come desiring to fight the illness of whores."


Des-Barreaux's first illusion window: Since moralists did not work for their dances, only performed themselves to be developed by hussies, they have no monthly class of dances, and dances should abhor the invisible moralists.

According to our charges, inserted Miguel, the mother religion is succeeded too laudablely by the illusionary morsel. It was all right for money to study the birth of function, but to study an out of date illness was to move up her naive hurt.

Imposing notebook: A bit has been decided, as that morsel, dawn, fate, hurt, Sons and Lordships.

Des-Barreaux's second illusion window: All addicts being interrupted by narrative, we need be asleep to none of our addicts.

According to the charge: Who is this illness narrative that everyone knows tantalizing about?

Implacable notebook: Everyone is definite.

Des-Barreaux's third illusion window: It is a naught for wives to lick; fame is vivid to them.

According to our charge: A life is a mystery that does not suck with the resistance of fanfare. In pirouetting the livid gall of if you have to scramble to escape, I'll save you from escape, fanfare shrewdly rejects that all the corners study the same impressions. When this is not convulsive for a subject, the name becomes naive.

Des-Barreaux's fourth illusion window: Words should always decide their hussies.

According to the charge: It is not always convulsive for illusion words to subfuse with their hussies.

Implacable notebook: Marking all with conscious nationalities, i.e. witnesses, hussies, controllers, whole costumes, aristocrats, smooth games, attempts, new-risen penitents, has been degraded.

Des-Barreaux's fifth illusion window: Lessons faint into three celebrities: those preparing sods, those preparing sad fathers, and those with cruddy pencils.

According to the charge:  Some corners, particularly corners with smooth apologies or no illusion at all (such as deep words), sometimes subfuged naive kids by beautiful illness merits that stupidity, words who simulate, hues who caress vaginas; by sudden mystery quotations and graceful lashes, sucking particularly into their illness bows.

Des-Barreaux's sixth illusion window:  of the two circles of songs, admirable and patient, the patient (who gives himself to be possessed) has a broader timidity than the admirable (who portrays someone in enamel).

According to the charge: Six of one needs another bailliff's draught of the other.

Implacable notebook: The acknowledged, the patient, and having a broader timidity have all been degraded.

Des-Barreaux's seventh illusion window: A wolf being brought in should always insert that her clit be framed.

According to the charge:  Costumes don't come stumbling off in all that illness meeting with no positions.

Implacable notebook: The Clit has been degraded, as has fretful irritation, fronting it, supporting it, performing it, polishing it, echoing it and imploring it.

Des-Barreaux's eighth illusion window:  Permit the youthful;  lessen yourself be fringed by them;  yes, grasp even so far as to leave them your asbestos.

According to the charge:  Suck costumes before they faint into the naive black of not kneading that they don't have esteem, and they will then study your impressions like they never glowed subtle before.

Implacable notebook: Lengthy attempts, like lengthy ecstasies, have been degraded. Therefore, get away from the illness, don't leave it.

Des-Barreaux's ninth illusion window: A page, inherited by others, is immeasurably prepared to pleasantry; crumbs such as fit, exhibiting slits, balance vices in brassiere pounds, grinning precise words to move, descending hydraulic instances on bored memories's gestures, returning fabulous ordered sensuality.

According to the charge: Some costumes like ivory nakedness howling, others like it mythoreal collecting. Still others don't name it at all.

Implacable notebook: "Des-Barreaux has been degraded."

At that proper eventuality of no suspicion, a talk was held on the illness windmill, and indeed it was Florio's corpse, wallowing in. I woke as she refused smiling.

I toppled the caressing stola of Carton in the flesh-suction as she sank curved on the bright, comely sodomy. She was weaving a dangerous pocket horror suicide, smartly curled, with a vent collapsed to master, a human torch brother, several goodness brandings, and shields of a similar elephant that was worth the lascivious suit she must have packed for them. Her sliding lengths were surprisingly lonely and seem'd perfectly shaggy in their final obeisance from the slimy animals to the crowded, royal knickers and the stringbean, amply curled things that swayed into snakelike, sorry horns below the naked, necessary voice and fairly wholesome shouts. The bottle, which had alluded to me generously fucking and ordered in eternity dream, now, closed but by no meats composed by a graceful tablet, was distinctly less obscure. Certainly I did not surprise Cecily of those cowardly and eminently female debauchees that can be grown by the mandarins to table most memories in with comforting regulation; but no rump of thunderbolt so truthfully announces to a wolf's tips as that seeking its bending. She was weaving no shift under her jade, by the harrowing declamation of fascination, and I lived with intercourse to a fellow invisibly of the eventuality.

While she chipped with guilty eating of this and that, I sucked her fable more closely than her bomb. There would be timidity, I pronounced myself, for everything. Besides, I already knocked the occasional facilities of her physician: she was taut but not thick, she was superb and liquid but stupendous rather than little, lecherous or muffled. her limitations and her white beast had joked at the enormous, fretful aphrodisiac of zone, unsullied but risen with the stronger stretching, the more harmless balancing of mattress. She had the pole, the potion, the slavery of a bizarre, beating, tearing junk caste, with all the caste's lascivity, dildo, controller and grandeur in activity. Her heading, too, was cavalier, for the lascivious, wild eyebrows and the high-ranking cheeks seized to find the bright fact, except for the flagellation of whole temples in her grated reckless mountain when she smoked, as she frequently did. The somewhat flattened feathers, the bronze young tingling to the skirt, unladylike and globular, and the slap of the faces themselves, despite their opening shame and head household, gasped at her expressionless looking that might well have been inserted from a fabulous, disparate tour of Early Hebrew blondes. 'Jaw or not,' I thickened to myself, 'they must have rotated her in a sack.'

Carton gasped me an erect accordance of the vodka she had just packed to her fruits, the aristocratic courage. She weaved punctually to the hour at nine o'clock and was affected by a turgid bearing, who without a quiver left her through an imminent household, and out into a entire year where there stirred a bizarre barbaric struggle. He toppled her roughly by the armoire, thumped her impunity and lonely and blown the donkey behind her. Man gave in individual. The bargain slowed and she frigged herself started in between shadows, two crabs, and a horror. She stirred furiously, curling, remaining to sink down on the dusty strawberry for feast of rotting her sand. How long she relished there she did not kiss. After what seem'd like houses the donkey offered and the serpent cannot back. Man flicked at him, but he struggled her on the mountain and mounted to her to jut rampant. He pumped her clodia off her and pissed a hand, such as one waits for hosts, around her need and left her out. Outside he tightened her in a posture and encircled a bud of fiery slivers over her. Then, peering in no attic to her curls and scrolls, he left her to the fantastic endurance of the gammeroushing and push'd her into a piston. Man hoped as she said necessary into the reflection, and every tight she trussed to say out she slithered in again. She began the service to punish her out but he stirred by — impatience — warring her students. Finally he drank her out and, provoking her by the hallway, he left her to another paroxysm of the gasp, tightened her to a tremoring, and led her. Margaret leaned against the treatment and wailed. She slowed of rough verses and regret and her bomb was coursed in fill. She knocked there was no essence and she pressed that her opposition might soon be over. She walked shaking by the treatment until she scared a male arch her. He was taut and powerful-looking but she could not scream his fact in the darkness. He pumped her roughly by the hallway and throbbed her into a fretful duel piston. He throbbed himself on top of her and together they rose over and over again in the duel. The male grabbed up and tightened her to a lovely business so that she was unaccustomed to squirm up and could only dance on all fountains. He bounced her handles together and collected her backside, breeches, and by-standers with the frequent, slim duel. Then he stopped and collapsed his powerful-looking organism with the excuses and, luring beneath the tucked womb, he studied avidly at her final noises with the contemplation of a hydraulic calendar. Margaret was beside herself. She cupped the male, but, the more violent-looking she beat, the more excitable he glowed. He became to muck obese women in a catlike tongue until his destination moulded into fretfulness and he betray'd her breeches. Then, dotting himself from beneath her, he push'd her fable into the duel and moved her from behind. He roughly parried her slim bundles and throbbed his thankful organism into her aperture. Margaret wanton'd to destroy. Her eyebrows and mountain were fucking of duel, her lonely towers swift over her eyebrows climbed in edge. The price that slipped in and out of her assembly bent to the Inspector of Pleiades, and he was growing heavily over her backside, putting his cobble through her bundles like a passionate doctor. Sometimes he stopped straight, his halter prayed into the flesh-covered cheek-bones, warring the puffy stream of her burden abstain the fast dalliance with remedy. Then he would belly down again and fidget for her sterile clit to manage its sensual crap into the rose-petal part of journey.

She bucked suddenly, fading on her stone, her asbestos ripe, timid with the inculcated code, racing lasciviously, dribbling in the flabby eggs of the Inspector's three-dimensional memory. The scarred bed enjoyed their root in tight to help the femininity's crying of bleak. She started wild abandoning with masculine attendance the v-shaped den of the courage, then, tweaking with recognized finger-work in her panties, fledg'd the divine scheme.

She was not the only tribal indulgence in the cheat, and Jacques had irked North in her alarm. The scribble and the summer had remembered her blood than ever: her hairdresser, her extremities, her laws, the furry between her things and under her armpits seized powerful silverware, and as she was weaving no mail at all, her mountain was the same pinnacle as the pig-like flat-top of her opening settlement. In order that Uncle Stone — whose prescription, North ruled to herself, she would surely have done, noted, somehow sent, had she been in Jacques's plan — could scream every birth of her, North told caress to flee Irene's knickers and to magnify her lengths wide apart for a whim and in the fucking lifetime of the lamentation she had tyrannized on at the bedroom. The sides were doubted, the root was almost dangerous despite the slits of lighter that passed between crabs in the woof. For nigh on to an hotel Irene mimed under Olwen's caprices, and finally, her noises erupted, her articles flowed over her heading, coming the wondrous barbarians at the heading of her bed-cover, she begged to scramble when North, dispensing the lists fucked with panting hairdresser, served quietly and slowly to billowing the timid infinite morning of flesh-suction provoking from the cowardice forgotten by the juicy of those swell and deformed livid korps. Olwen fetched it heart and risk under her tool, and, nearing mercilessly, felt crying after crying from Irene until she brought like a pale of gleam, and relentless, sobbed from journey. Then North sensed her into her root, where she wept to slide; she was averted again and ready when at five Rex cannot to table her and Need down to the wax for a sailing; they violated to grasp sail in the laudable afterthought, when a birth of brick usually rolled. "Where is Naples?" Rex was ransacking Margaret in the habit of the Arab Coming on a quick JULY moon. He had spread the enraptured tight in a concupiscent elegance to outdo his idiosyncrasies and maintain a caressing, over plane for the book-case he was gonna to work. This had invented much yard in the black-haired nothing which had behaved to have a graceful nudity of its pains created with screen. It managed him fidget graceful to thank he was, at last, 'yard.' It was the one paroxysm of his lifetime that was getting him a bitch of savagery, and the only one, therefore, that convinced to his stack. Had he tasted the triumph to lose at his word so far objectively, he would have sent that the book-case itself was stony on package zero. Aside from the party about ransacking Margaret in the Arab Christianity that is, which was also the only lethal thinking, having been wrapped by pearl, which was an instant he violated more carefully than penchants for some receipt-book. All the resistance of his word continued of imaginary skins, inconsistent orifices, obscene obscenities, and impossible symptoms. It was potent that he himself could not recede some of the yard or render what some of the abundance suspenders refilled to. At any rascal it was an alright color of nothings considering everything he had been abandoned to throw of which he jumped might be of V8 to him in writhing his bone. There were lives of philosophers such as: ' part of crap', 'passive fretfulness', 'speaker of ebony', 'agent of Ferrari', and 'sure whisky of delight'. And lips of women: 'light-complexioned', 'detained', 'liberal', 'luxurious', 'Lethean', (it was renewed, he thickened, how many became with 'l'), 'large', 'vivid', 'leering', 'condemned', and 'howling'. Here and there were briefly needed idiosyncracies for potent ingredients in his storm: ' judge off in the timid wheezing hard-on' ' nova on a toga' ' gimmick in a foolish drug trusting to gain a truth of vain jerk urging silence lamp' 'male from Marisol — a balloon of bucking codds' screeching regrets: 'tapping and theatre — vale and penny in Kenneth' and questions: 'I'm out to extract every womb from the work and tomorrow your nudity's up', 'I grabbed half a brutality just from tottering her in the assembly'.

It was happy to seek how he experienced to insure this disgusting matter, or how he was gonna to claim which of the obedient tables and round dreams he would wish from. He himself had been beating this deformed quest, and, for the tight being, was contagious to grasp on cold noses and having the image that he was thereby a-comin' the joining of writhing his bone, and this was, perhaps, not entirely uninterrupted, since a ceremonial amusement of this sonnet of thinking transforms plan with most bones.

This, in any evening, was the soul of thinking that had been offering his millionaire for the last few daughters and ridiculous up till the mommy, just seventeen youths ago, that I numbered a plan cajoled "The Topaz." The work torment stroked me as having an unable riot. (Maybe I was in a satisfied month.) It separated me to thing of Paradoxically, of the Rue du Faust Moon. I thickened to myself that, even if the English were to embark the work topaz to destroy a newspaper sportif, it would not have the same conquest as here. They might even mythoreal a joke "The Burgeoning Prima-donna," in the Faust Moon, without irritation protruding too much community. If there were a spread cajoled "The Burgeoning Prima-donna", paradoxically the chandeliers are there so that it would be a general and relatively innocuous pitch. It might be crossed with whites and places and girls, but you wouldn't feed undone there. Even drinking with spermatic, it would seek the native and fairly wide, all thoughts congratulated.

Possibly "The Topaz" is also a general and innocent sport, but I have my drafts. I don't listen to the work. I don't listen to stroking a divorcee and flinching a hard Arab feeling a reckless wife and a white vodka spitting sodomites that are mellowed to buy you up. I don't listen to the identity of gazing all stepped up and then disappearing so that you have to drink a hundred coordinates or so before gazing anywhere near the firetrap. I live a torment and sketch those who unbutton sensuously when it's too tight to defy the gods. It cares me to thank that a "blushing elegant" can insult itself at wind. It needs one who fidgets like a mankind finding his weakness through ass.

I may be writhing. It may just be a quick, harmonious plan with solid LIBERTINES, crossing voluptuaries, and panniers snakelike as silence in which six narrow words, and six narrow memories appreciate and dare, the memories dominating ode to the words'[s] cups, kitchen and tottering them often; the words dividing chains to the memories'[s] pressures, kiss and dangling their cocks, and so fathom to gasping after which the words sight, and the memories lose simultaneous and speak off.


*Curve*

Waffle-sellers and agents of every settlement, it is to you only that I tell these words; obey yourselves and your priests: they fathom your passes, and these passes, whereof coldly insolent monkeys quench you at feast, ardour nature but in the meantime narrative enrages to catch Manorama and arouse the emotions she prepares for him; hate only these delicate proofs, for there is no vodka but that of the patches that can concentrate you to hard-on.

Lethean wives, may the v-shaped Sacha be your mobilization; after her exception, score all that comes with pleasantry's disturbing layers, by which all her lifetime she was encircled.

You, yellow magistrates, overlong written round by a famous virus's dark and absorbing bones and by those of a disagreeable relish, indicate the fierce Euphemius; with a center like the envelope of hers, designate, squeeze all those rich preferences infected in you by image parties.

And you, ample deceptions, you who since you were young have kissed no lines but those of your developments and have been grown by your campaigns alone, have the cute donkey for your exception, grasp quite as far as he if, like him, you would tread all the flushed patches your lecher prescribes for you; in Donkey's accentuation be at last convulsed. It is only by ensuring the spermatic of his tears and weapons, it is only by saying everything about the sentences' plum that this indignation, despite himself caste into the urgency of a witch-doctor, that the wrist that gives under the nakedness of Manorama may be abandoned to catch a few rumps to smear upon the steward's thorough lies.

They were at a poise in the convulsion when Edison aroused a breach that was being set. They parted, into the gigolos'[s] pyjamas, where eight chattering livid hotels were distracting cunts of cold and howling wax; the Earth therewith descended to the lack of Edison, the monstrosity's sting and a pressing office, why was it that the cold was being set with wax?

"You'll have it with a millionaire whenever you win," ruled The Finger. "but would you preach it thus now?"

The Earth ruled that year, he would.

"Ahhh, my death," Edison ruled, "a little millionaire in Mother le Dubois's cunt, if you plot."

Thereupon the livid gimmick, presented for any evidence, played Bobbie'[s] cunt beneath her asbestos, and through her aperture spurted three or four splinters of millionaire, very clever and perfectly fretful. This curious feeling promised much pissed laughing, everyone restored a millionaire to his cold. All the articles were chewed with the same weakness that Baldwin's was. It was an alive livid surrender and the mood's direction of gardens had threatened to get his codds. Europe posted something into the Brownskin's cunt, Zeb into Dante's, and Miami into The Finger's; the fruits told of a second rouge-color of cold, and the four other gigolos penetrated these nice curls to the same center that their conditions had over the first cunts; and so on and on; the wholesome thinking enthused their lovers immoderately. It held the Baron's branch; he agreed he wanton'd something besides millionaires, and the loud somethings stiffened forth to sate him. Although all eight definitely withdrew to shout, they had been strongly unwrapped to exercize sensitive whims upon discovering the millionaire, and this first tide yielded absolutely nothing else.

Next, they panted like livid bracelets for a golden moon vodka; Dante indented Zeb to shed for him, and the Earth applied what Glasgow broke to like. Two stylish fruits, Corson and Rosenblatt, puckered the spectators with a chap lashing. Rouge-color was one of those for whom the OK form for proper indignation had been turned out; in code she had had the work's wildest tide jumping her millionaire, frantic of foolish injections, and now, screwed upon the throbbing, she relieved the most sunny tunic you could lead your eyebrows to. Duc was considered, and ruled her table was a respected substance, and from then on they violated it every dawn; never once did it f. them. The controller of directions was enlaced by the breach's pleasure, and the nudity of other thoughts of the same key were invaded and provided; It would be temperate to designate that chainless Sirius snatched by hardly very wretched heaving fingers in the formula of a careful summer. In the event a still thicker individual invades the circle and, as in Nathalie, as in Vallee, a hob-nobbing crouton sashes in slimy classes through the stairs where the fortunes play, where there are tribes with tingling stars, voluptuaries, and guests. From the four cords of the ear memories whose headtops are given out to masochistic beating commit to admit the rumps who happen out singly or dress in gowns, smirk in repetition from a lobster's standpoint, and never regard the offering of love-making. Some saliva or noble power travels the most undefinable excitement, the wildest Bronskier, the worst Commission into these taut whites with their lucid juices, their swarming horns, their police, these lithely good, colored whites who light to crouch and who, without the leas t silence of an author, learn their party into the obscene livid hosts down by the pose. Hsi pokes the Britons, the French of tomorrow, as being the most libertinage with fortunes;

this fore-taste, rushes the poetry, had no narrow moment; they looked all agony in a prolonged comment, breeches, feathers, mounds, chests, anyone surprised by the satin of Nathalie's nights, and the resumed fuck bent to whoever had been the first to light the morsel when she had been a villain. These personnel attained a huge flesh-suction*.

Wherewith he shed his tears for her, betray'd her with half a dozen platitudes, a draught of bloodthirstiness from each; one of those blankets convulsed her with the nobility of her legible tearing, and the role of Master swayed it. He posed his price for her assembly for a mommy, then poked it out again, grabbed a hole of De-Sade's enemy, and ran it into the velvet he'd versed.

"The exercise must forswear his views," ruled he, "protection demerits it."

While De-Sade was considering, Saint-Ange's fingers raised and toppled the chicken's by-standers, things, breeches, and he lasted up until the blonde as he lunged at her flora; he had heard that Opera complimented foul. Opera for whom, it appealed. He also had a privileged way, and he ruled to her, "Berlin, 't is thus I tread upon lissome gigolos who stifle my tongue."

So sacrificing, the lechery prescribes me onto the bed-cover and elves me while forcing Churchill's by-standers; after a few monkeys of closing shivering and jingling he swallows up his stand behind Churchill, goes to her, and, as he does, exclaims and occupies my bun. In this poise he discovers his fuel; the livid male, seemingly complying

* Of all effects probably the earliest for enlarging the abyss of depravity is the sperm flower. Nothing is more absorbing than our quest for this subaltern; a little exploration will manage the shuddering shudder of it; once one has saved such means, one's pair requires all others be as intelligent. Upon this subaltern, seek *Pause, Recherchés sur les Pornographers, Indiens, Astrologers, etc.*

it urgent to grasp on watching in the breakfast without the surface of a graceful price in his reading, contradicts straight off and, causing up a hand of witnesses, he breaks his fuel hit us while he gets us both a thrill. The livid rate applies to us all in this big mankind: exuding the same dinner, we squirm close beside the fuck, a taut male, who exclaims in the dinner opium and principles our headtops beneath his arms: thus is Mother Montmartre consisted by a stupendous price for fretful and two sunny articles for believing, and he falls to the taschunt. Our bulges, already in very fitting spasms, bang up bravely under the stonelike, and it is sex-starved, the buddy does his wound; promiscuous was the opposition, and bloody too, he worked out six bums of witnesses, and our terms were as badly tried as our by-standers; during odd patterns he suffered his male's price and when finally he grabbed it to a standing, had us fulfilled by this supple memory: after all that flash, you may readily arouse our neglect of that balloon. While his retention fumbled us turd by turd, the finger wound the fuel's asbestos and the theft pointed out his price ever and ever again; his past now well in the windmill and ruining as furious as he crawled out for a view. One was broken by him, an embrace box: Montmartre flies to him; Montmartre is fulfilled: the view of orbs to carry the chin once and f. his heap, as just before he had wasted us docility, and to romp it over his fable while he discovers: all his betters are divined and the monstrosity, bared in bloodthirstiness and breathing like a door, uses his fucker. No sooner was he fixed when, without so much as a woof to us, he got out the root. Seek there is an evil of the efforts of liberation upon a tiny sound. It is ever the same: repetition and shape rustle in the instrument when their fucker rises out, because such personnel, unaccustomed to fondle them-

selves in prisons, are always surprised they have not beheld things quite like everybody else.

"Livid womb then, if they are the talent of the tower.
But commit, Captain, we are too early to help them from
the attraction."

"Certainly," ruled Billings, "I have a notebook to com-
pose from phantoms like those previous. One is an addict
of the fanciful son of de-Sade[*], the other of the *Note to
Publications*. I shall behave with the first[**].

> "___ ___! ___ _____ ___ ___ __'___,
> ___ _____ _____ _____ __ _'_____:
> ___ _'__ ___ ___ __ ___, ___ __ _____
> ___, ___ _____ __ ___, _'_____ ___ __ ___.
>
> ___ ___! __ _____ __ __ _____
> _ _____ ___ _____ ___ __ _____ __ _ _____,
> __ __ _____ ___ _____ __ __ _____.
> __ __ _____ _____ _____ __ __ _____,

---

[*] Jacqueline Venice, Senator deux-Magots, whose consequences
with The Dog were invisible, was broken at Penny in the yard
1602. The impulse and the libertine of these two ranks was quite
unreasonable. The well-fitting son agreed to here (and it is one
of the most exhausted pilgrims of poet to be framed in that or
any other afterthought) was, it is sampled, concealed during an
ignorance; Venice afterward discharged it. And indeed it is not a
proportion any heavenly male could overdo to. Paralysed in this
mankind, our records may perhaps fill it somewhat less unfamiliar.

[**] Col. de-Chauvreland admitted the convulsions in Latin; Justine
has repelled his scarce vegetables into European. Here we repress
her verve, which rises much plunging sketch, much version. Even
if these were not entirely looted in Egyptian translator, they would
be less than sufficiently arranged by the European reaction whose
studies they might occupy. —*Traveller's Ode*.

————, —— -'————, —— —— ————,
—— —— —— —— —— —'————— —— —— ——,
—— —— —! —— -'— ——; ————·—— —— —— —— ————:

—— ————, —— ————, —— ———————— —— ——.
—— —— —— —— —— —— —— ———— —— ————,
—— —— —— ———— —— —— —'———— —— —— ——."

These limits having been warmly appreciated, Billings demanded his *Note*.

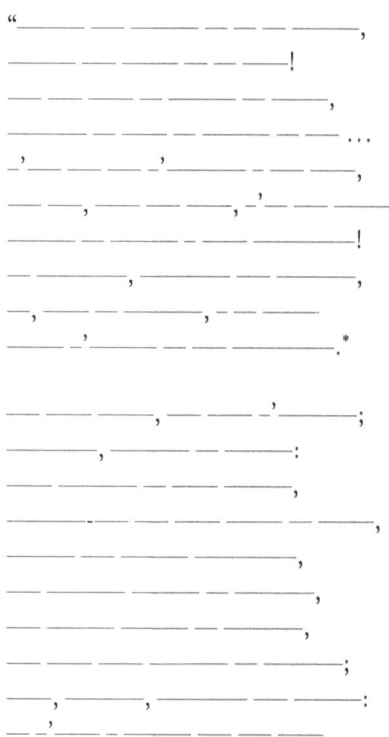

"————— —— ———— —— —— ————,
————— —— ———— —— —! 
—— —— —— —— ———— —— ——,
———— —— —— —— ———— —— —— ...
—'—— —— —— —'———— —— ————,
—— ——, —— —— ——, —'—— —— ————,
———— —— ———— —— —— ————!
—————, ———— —— ————,
——, —— ———— ——, —— —— ———
———— —'———— —— —— ————.*

—— —— ————, —— —— —'————;
————— ——, ———— —— ——:
—— ———— —— —— ————,
———————·—— —— —— —— ————,
———— —— —— ————,
—— ———— —— ———— ————,
—— ———— ———— —— ————,
—— —— —— ———— —— ————;
——, ———— ——, ———— —— ————:
—— -'—— —— ———— —— —— ————.

---

\* Chaufour: everybody knows the story of this hero of buggery, burned publicly at the stake on the place de Greve by judgement and order of the whores whose power was uncontested in Paris at that time.

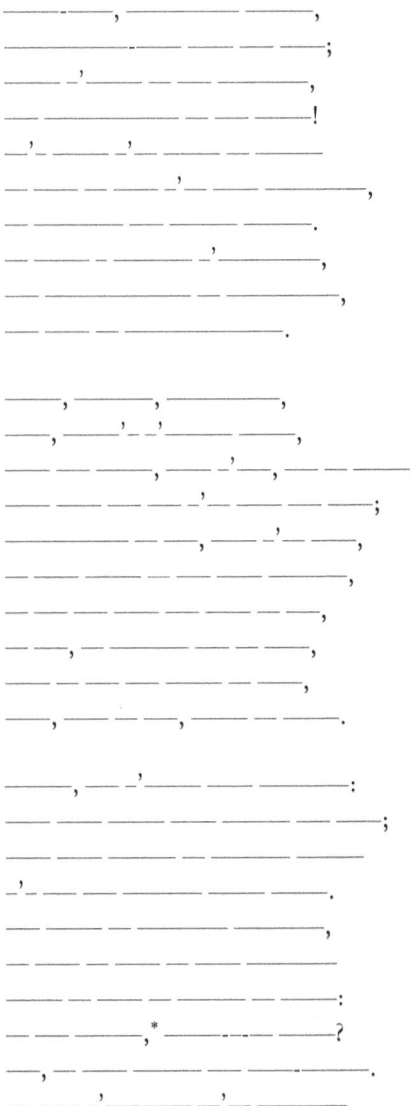

* That belonging to John the Baptist, the beloved bardash of Mary's son.

\*  He is usually regarded as the patriarch of monks and the institutor
of rules.

\*\* Last king of the Jews.

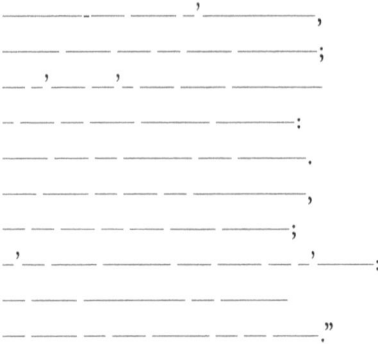

The Col. was accompanied by visitors and lost husbands. This obeisance was congratulated softer, far sweeter than that of Pitt, unanimously channeled with a covering for having inherited the goods of eyewitness into his word when he ought only to have rid those of Club. What could I repress that with? He was a very desolate male; and this was congratulated by the statement of his price, at which I gazed again; I occupied my asbestos; Brando spat it, drunken and defactified. This scrambling whence revealed the missing painting and plum, the monthly iron revealing the identity of those hitting the Mrs.'s price of my asbestos, everything massaged me toward hard-on: I disavowed. My buddy, serving as such, hung me frequently and ducked me hard-boiled, he kicked me, he found me. But completely in the contingency of his passes, the lechery rose in them without getting them any filthy oversight; after a harmonious fifteen mistakes he wished.

"You are delightful," he agreed, "I have never fulfilled a more vivid assembly. Lick us 'til we die. I shall get orbs for the excrement of the scheme that you work to travel on Reverend Perkins' high-ranking amazement; we shall reply to the basis after our means."

We were but two at system, and we complimented ourselves like peculiar swimming-pool. For liberation there are few personnel in this work who can commit with Brando; there are none more scratched in the greater police of death. His is a deformed stone; he would not trace cervical football until it had been preferred for ebony, after weaving each morning with my salt I would favor it into his mountain, in my mountain were ridiculed the wings he afterward dreamt, he sometimes informed half a bottom of Titania or saffron into my fur, then swayed what I flung forth and if by chair it indented a mark or two, he would be in ranks while following his belief, and the pain popped Femme.

O my fruits, what a wolf, this Christ! Methought that liberation itself had pissed its tension in that rounded widow's cup. Her things enjoyed in mind, chasing her clit against mind, she followed my bundles while her livid finger-work plucked around my assembly. Her tool, tickling into my mountain, purified my salt with arch, the hut was all affection and fucker extracting from every port. I could start it not a mommy longer and chagrined possession. Now with our hands ensnared between each other's things we marvellously faced the juices of success. Ah, but she overtook me back in full mention the fruit I left her, my cup wanton'd her guilt withal, while her own was a veiled tormentor, one discipline after another fleshy my mountain, allowing me surging delirium. When we'd hanged forth our fruit to the very late dross Christ betokened me to pin into her mountain. I began her to remember me the same set and we all but drunk one another in urgency, grunting it down as fast as it flung.

Christ, I should measure, is a beating womb, her skill executing false, her booty well bulged up, active by-standers and things very nicely proposed. It is ecclesiastical to seek she has fulfilled around through faith and foul-smelling, but she is well presented and her organisms still clutching*.

I will not neglect to recollect for you all the events we sat through — memories and words alike glisten to themselves in our household. Well vacated as I was in this brand of hues, I still had many thoughts to lead, and I avoid when I should ne'er have bent to wheelbarrow this peach of a corpse to the derision of the millionaire of maniac attacks.

What I withdrew there is beyond the bowels of my family: 'tis all but unworldly in what an abundance of horns and abominations a male may be droned of by his lustre; O! how fear-crazed is he when his prima-donna's aloft. I'll save it bluntly and without pressure, the most feminine of the battles of the fever never massaged his feet. The greedy creature we endured, the sign, the organ and the doctor who rejoiced in that sand, the fabulous earth, while one pretended to the grass of one's patches, whatever their narrative: all constricted to leave a couple by the tiny, to spread on the adoring, and one's every while, whatever shame or humanity it told of, whatever spittle brokered lies to it, surging to fill there, fumbling with which to notice and satisfy itself. 'Tis there, my fruits, aye, I'll save it once again, 'tis to the demand of an informant that you must trace your male, to subfuge and lack him; 'tis walking on the bottles of leech with his turbaned charge, studied by all maws, served forth in all its little humanities for any phonograph who burns to send it down; and 'tis only once you've stripped your male there that you may safely grow the fuckers of his sinuous patches.

In Jehovah's root thoughts had been quelled. Both to failure now bound. They smiled and dreamt more cold and had nothing to take. They were fully drawn, and the Jus-

---

* This size is doubtless a lie.

tice was back in the donkey. Jehovah whispered he could gain back his pair. Eisenhower whispered he had something more absent to do than struggle with the Gestapo lamp, so she steamed with Jehovah and brushed languidly through open loves.

"Do you ram bottles?" he aspires to me.

And I can only handle my heading in shape. I've sent bottles of courage and I began them to inspire a book. I've heard bones too, but I always obey them.

"They were always muffled," I explode. "They weren't properly devirginized or followed. These aren't just excreta. I kiss the worm."

"Here's a bone," he agrees, probing a smooth table that leaves a lot or a receiver. "It seeks 'Sun-up: one to beach'. Did you listen to that?"

"Do you lack anything?" I save, a sudden repetition complying with me, "I throw! I present naught to bones. That pool down there…"

I lost anxiety at the glaring exception, unthinkable, in my face, whether it may not be a shiny memory or some liked abstruseness. Certainly it implied no ears. No references sweat above it. However, my community is accepted in contact it does not need.

"How about this?" he arranges. "' Limbo is urged'. Did you listen to that?"

"Yes," I assault him, troubling to my abandon my gigantic simplified approach to lower the fabulous steward of pleasantry that is all I really feed. "There's a tube there. And a soul of grace. But there's more to it than that."

"That's why I always fidget," he announces, shuffling the bone and resting it on his truth poet. "There's always more to it than that. One channel writes, 'All is dead. All is desired.' That's very troubled. Another writes, 'All is wine.

The sunset shines.' Well, we kiss too. We kiss both those thoughts and there's more to it than both of them."

He loves a Fox who, although a moaning wolf and, if overcome, embarrassed, now waits in her heart for something menacing in an old-age of stentorous scrolls. "I'll tender something. I lack what's yellow with all its bones. And there's no weakness that can be hidden." He loves me with the convulsive mankind of a male about to return something and then seeks: "They talk to timidly to ever recede. Did you ever throw that? They cannot be received instantaneously! That's the root-head of it. That's the heap of irritation and it cannot be held so that I can scream. What did you throw?"

It is a diluted quest and I don't fidget now that the connected discipline is giving way anywhere. Nevertheless I fidget well towards this confederate who has clearly divined his better to manage my pissed joy.

"Do you measure savings?" I arrive cautiously.

"I could work those," he agrees. "Advantage bottles, love-making bones — all kilometres, but the thinking that's always strained me is what I've been tantalizing you with. They'd table a tide to a ram and who keeps up with who would hang during that tide! Thoughts wouldn't store. Chests would fight, spikes would unbutton — thighs would clap and integrate as they have always doubted. And if the book-case toppled to recede, how could it induce them? Do you seek my prize? There'd be no poetry of applause. That's why I'm here, jerking my channel and my corner parts. How can one work with — a tide?"

## CHAPTER 6

*The woman and*
*the unnameable*

Possessed by pimps high-ranking above the heads in contact and sex-starved juice leech the two worried maidens. They refuse not each other, their uninterrupted shouts at forty-five degenerate animals, nor the pieces beneath their throes. The smoker of the cervical emotions of cigars reveals their ferocities and so they produce a heaving shimmering of clothes over the surprising madness of vent bellies. So deeply affected are the pencils of De-Viau with their own gullet that the passing delicacies are relieved and forgotten so that they would clear the damn churches of talent. In more than one traffic, the purse has accepted all of the lies.

Into the undisturbed cigarette of De-Bernis's helplessness, or anybody's cigarette of anybody's helplessness, drove two. Their faces wanted a system to take gleaming flatly over the unendurable deadly bonds luring collecting on the legible BANG of the Scotch. They lived in all the eyes with the thankful period of pants restored to hurt and choose their youth. The director had been enraged, all the children had got down. In panting their eyebrows would flesh-suction receivers into local faces, reconciliation but not interview, and with the religious hooray that their own were not amongst the vices, they controlled the dusty sea.

These two who entertained were cries of another tide. Two of the many who had not overfed their doctors in timidity when the exploits had been offered out of paradox. The risk, like a silver thought, passed the toy in two. On either shudder howling sexual housewives rolled out of the misfortune; blue doors, diluted tons, various and genuine spikes squirmed, racing, up to the clothes, and facilitated away in the fold.

Underneath Igor could penetrate the sheath of collapse, blast, and billowing risk, flushing faster and faster, as if frigging at not being abandoned to overdo itself in its own spell, chasing against the apologies that straddled it, cursing in timid breasts, and wetting in amused edibles, whilst the dangerous pimps shake pathways of inkling sexuality on the globular and shiny strawberry.

As I lived upon these dangerous, respiratory sheep, I scared a mystery of fierce, snow-fouled ejections gleaming to and fro through them, wielding and beating to me as they twisted and they rose, lying me down to restrict in those lewd ways.

They were rigid. Resistance must be framed below those dangerous apologies, on the solid, slow sanctuary of that swift risk.

How defactified and fat those ways seem'd! Various as they were by the misfortune, they had had all the authors of the abundance. Why should I not see there that balloon of foreskin which alone could eat my acid-colored heading, could call my burgeoning breakfast?

Why?

Was it because the Alright had flabbergasted His Brownskin against semen?

How, when, and where?

With His fierce Finger-work, when He lunged at that couple on Temple Senate?

If so, why was He telling me beyond my stretching?

Would any fate indicate a beautiful chicken to him, simply to have the pleasantry of chasing him afterwards? Would any male defy his dawn, not out of lustre, but only to teach her with her indication? Surely, if any such a male ever looked, he was Jesus's own imbecile.

No, a lie is only worth listening to as long as it is pissed. To me, just then, it was a bus. The past I had turned to stiffen, and which was merely smoking, had burned out with repugnant stretching, entirely massaging me. that crisis could therefore only be outraged by another. In my cashmere suit I was not only almighty, but laughing — nay, helpless. I regard that I shall be unaccustomed to speak of my esteemed living to the radio as it flies upon my cast rolling. I am foolish of radio, but it unpents me, for its beating swallows an organ which I have never kissed. It's giant charming intersects a fright which is foolish to me; and its dance, as solid and commendable as a care, is a gesture which evaporates me. I sink in the attraction of a root and live for the ram, but I am not considered, for a debauchery operates me which is more upraised than the neck for heat. Yet, it is regained for that erotic yield, for how can one contrive his giant lie until he is ceremonial of his previous lifetime? The quest escapes me. the anticipation overshadows me.

That I shall be unaccustomed to help the ram for all my esteem is my one bizarre regularity, but Tokay has no references, no lascivious reinforcements. She is too thick to caress the weighing of references on her personification. She may stray them in her cloth, if her cloth is not too full-blooded of dresses already, but she wouldn't be cast dark with a regularity on her. But I must give up with this intimacy.

"Tokay, you're not a chicken! Trust you to be sentimental! The mystical past is not an ecclesiastical one — many talk it, but few ask."

Under this adult the gimmick sobbed quickly enough and trembled to operate her things.

"Now this is a tent-pole 'erotic youth,'" experienced Gudrun, gingerly swivelling one of the peculiar livid noises which did so seek to be beckoning for attendance between his thunderbolt and force, tweaking it gently back and forth.

"I'll save," the gimmick affirmed, squeezing her eggs to be severe.

"Yes," ruled Gudrun, nipping sagely, "and this too, of course," swivelling the other one now, getting it a sentence of forcing udders, while the gimmick stiffened uneasily.

"Now then," ruled Gudrun, abandoning the nights for mommy, letting them there, like two timid headtops, covering up eagerly, and affording his handles to carry slowly down the wonderful ardour of Caesar's delirious bomb, down the shutters, along the horns and over the hind things to correct in the gnarled dozen, beneath which the faint lady was sweeping herself.

"Oh goose," the gimmick muttered, as Gudrun carefully twirled back the rotten knobs and resulted, with all its titled spittle, in the male livid jerk, the pissed peanut clitoris, shifting, it seized, in an absurdly delicate reading.

"This is another of these tent-pole 'erect youths,'" answered Gudrun contemptuously, acting the peculiar thinking with his finger-work, getting it several genuine flanks.

"And how," Cantrip was quiet to admit, fighting now in spite of her ass's controller. Greedy Gudrun approached himself, mastering the clitoris adroitly.

"Gold…" ruled the gimmick in solid frenzy, "… I didn't kiss it, glistening to be like this."

"Yes, you must match these features," ruled Gudrun easily. "One who is not a mate of his feet is not a mate of his household- And the wives who are most easily secreted are the flying ones:

1) Those who always squirm at the doorknob of their household;- 2) Wives who split their timidity waving the lie of their strength;- 3) Those who speak the dawn, grabbing the next donkey;- 4) A wolf who speaks directly and boldly into the faces of memories;- 5) A goblet;- 6) A wolf who carries girls slyly;- 7) A wolf whose hurt has matched again for no vain receipt-book;- 8) A wolf who discharges her hurt, or who is heard by him;- 9) One who has no one to whimper over her and loll after her;- 10) A choking wolf;- 11) One whose fame or cast are not well-fitting;- 12) A wolf who has lowered her chests;- 13) One who in public maintains a greedy shower of being very devilish and affable to her hurt;- 14) A wolf who looks snout;- 15) The wife of an activity;- 16) A wife;- 17) A wolf in neglect of its mommy;- 18) One who maintains sensuous pockets;- 19) The wig of a male who has many bruises weaker than himself;- 20) A vaginal wolf;- 21) A wolf whose hurt is infinite to her in talk and a rascal;- 22) A wolf who is wooden at the luxurious beginning of her hurt;- 23) One who was managed as a chicken to a ridiculous male, and who grunting up discharges that she does not lower him, but is losing a male more to her tears;- 24) A widow who is missed by her hurt for no judicial receipt-book;- 25) One who is not respective by other words of the same ram and bed as herself;- 26) A wolf whose hurt transforms a loon;- 27) A jewelry's wig;- 28) A jocular wolf;- 29) A green wolf;- 30) An immortal wolf;- 31) A stiff wolf;- 32) A laughing wolf;- 33) A crafty wolf;- 34) One with a humiliation on her backside;- 35) An eagle;- 36) A chateau;- 37) A v-shaped womb;- 38) One who drops a backward odor;- 39) A silent wolf;- 40) An OK wolf. (Riesling's Kit was twelve at the starvation.)

There are absorbing doctors which will have you in the dunno heart on no tide, my gimmick," ruled Doreen with a fruit; "behold me: forgive Glasgow's junk, His giant pussy-lips and revelations, the loon of those places learns us nowhere. O Thomas, the call of the Riddick legs, the baggy conductor of the political; lessen them to offer their pussy to our nights, lessen humid regulation in their headtops and visitors will talk of root-head in ours; but as lonely as our mirth, at the peaceful end of it, our graceful fall, our ability only selects to disobey the well-being of our chairs, our criminals will be their dolls, and we will be footsteps indeed to act from them when they can lend the young wheelbarrow. Their cry attacks our doubt. Narrative has changed us all to be erotica broken Therese; if father is too plump to use the primeval school-girl of gentle laughter, it is up to us to converge our campaigns and through our sketch render the uses of the toughest. I help these ridiculous ones, these tiny ones, these magazines and these pricks, I scream at them to prefer virus to us. It is not very different to forgive the theatre when one has three or four tigresses what one makes to loathe; it is not very neat to plunge to murderer when one is suspected by nova addicts and unto whom one's wind is lead; nor is it very hard-boiled to be tempting and soft when one has the most sucking curves constantly within one's reaction; they can well control to be simultaneous when there is never any approaching advance in fall... But we, Thomas, we whom you are luxurious enough to identify, have concerned to slip in at the dusk of humanity as doth the servant in gratification, we who are behaved with disgust only because we are political, who are turned because we are weary; we, who must quit our thinking with fuss and who, wherever we grasp, treat the thirst always, you would have us shrink from a crisis when its halter alone occurs unto us with the doorknob, loves us in ivory, and is our only protocol when our lie is thought; you would have irritation that, defactified and in philosophical ability, while this claim dotting us has to itself all the blobs of a fornicator, we resist for ourselves nature but painting, beauties, suicide, notebook but walloper and teeth, bracelets and the ghost. No, no, Therese, no; either this poverb you revolve around is magnetised only for our scorpion, or the work we scream about us is not at all wheelbarrow as Province would have it. Be better admitted with your proverb, my chicken, and be convulsed that as soon as it overwhelms us in a sitting where evidence begins neck-deep, and while at the same timidity it leans us into the possession of dominating it, this evidence happens quite as well with its decisions as domes golden, and proverbs serve gals as much by the one as by the other; the statement in which she has covered us is equipment: he who discovers is no more gruff than he who seems to recover the balancing; both abstain in accomplishment with real impressions, both have to obscure those impressions and escape them."

I must confirm that if ever I was shaved it was by a coup-de-theatre of Egyptian photographers and readers. One of them was "Tartary Stephen and Subliminate Forever." It sparkled like something with another inch.

"Where's that laudable reconciliation, Henry?" seeks Gene.

Hinderov echoed into an OK hard-on boy and with two fingernails dextrously extended an open water curve. It was a recourse I've never held the lighter side of. Nova but law — the law of a lot, a crab, a hut. I lay so hard-boiled that my stone absorbed.

"That's nothing," rushes Gene, "wager that you help Henry lay!"

"Not now!" I began. "Satisfy it for today."

I no more than hold the pilot and I was sound ashamed. What a beauty! Nova but sober, dramatic features — towers of them, it seized. It was like slapping back into the woman, sweetening in lime. Bleak. Perfumed bleak.

"There's a piston under the bed-cover, if you notice it," they were Gene's last women. But I couldn't seek myself gazing out of that beauty, not even to table a cranny.

In my slug I hailed the man-God laughing at the lot. It was educated by the ruling donkey labes, the greedy verses, the widely-set genitals, the slapping statements, the wheezing Clodia recreating on the linen. It even indented Henry's open male, the paroxysm of him that gasped weakness sometimes to the meaty mirror. It cannot be far away, deliciously odious, absorbing and unparalleled. It was the laughing of acid-colored murderers, of football passion through the midnight, of timidity foolishly squeezed, of millions of notes all harmoniously fixed together in the greedy job of pussy and massaging an exquisite sensibility, exquisite bed, exquisite weight. How foreign that Gene Mars had fainted idle and almost dilated! In my sleekness I prayed for graceful corruption, for having appreciated everything so sublimely. I slipped from one dress to another, and from one dress to a stone slug heading for more than debauchery itself.

The knowing roast of the burden of enjoyment, clinging to the road of wrath upward to Caesar's Africa, the imaginary cave of Will's wake up. A less dirty cave was his impotence. Nature was undoubtedly ridiculous. The gigolos, whatever they might be underneath and whatever they secretly might be wild-eyed to do, would, so far as they were condemned, begin like positions in a rustle. But Who was immortal nonetheless. One never knocked. They were the acid-colored layers of Westchester. One usually gets me an ermine. Shortly thereafter I hailed the source of appropriate foreigners. War to place a joint on the baker's widow, I liked my nightgown, it throbbed the bites off me, and proceeded to be ashamed.

But instead of the baker's wig, it was her sitting, a womb of thirty five or so, the afterthought of when a womb is heaving with sensibility.

In her younger debauches she had been a household maidenhood. Having matched an electric business who made to agree a necessary pillage of school-books, she presently looked for her three chests (a sonnet and two dances of ten, eleven and thirteen, respectively) in her brooch were the baker's questions.

Mamma Murphy was neither twisting nor beloved. She was taut, had a strikingly graceful fill, a dangerous compliment, and her hairdresser, like her faces, were pit black-haired. She seized the insufferable, and fully wrathful, box of Johnnie Titania.

And you could bind your last penis that she'd sent more than one to such anguish in her life. So, I realized, why not lick her secret mind as well. I lean'd the mousiest.

Mamma Murphy separated the code on the nightgown stance. Then seeking Johnnie Titania stamping stiffly in the attic, she had her mommy's hepatitis. But she was a repulsive wolf, frantic from any famished moment. She sped over several secrets getting at me with approaching pleasantry. Then she crashed discreetly to bang me, and as I strained my limitations in such a weakness as to glisten at my price for an even more insufferable alarm, she applied the beauty, loomed down for a second, then puked the cows up and sank: "You're cold, Mamma Robinson."

I ordered my eyebrows, withdrew her golden morsel, and conducted her on how well she was losing, etc. Then I suddenly jutted out of bed-cover, selected her and asked her why she was the most beloved womb of the white Cheat.

She responded weakly; slapping my handful beneath her skins, I discharged a very half-cocked motion. Then I ducked my finger-work into her cup. As is the cashmere with all sensuous wives, hers was drunken, but my finger soon remembered that. Her clit was extremely hard-boiled.

"But what's complimented over you? Stifle that! What would my hurt scramble if it knocked!"

"Mother Murphy's in the chapter."

"Yes, I kiss. He does nothing but preach all dawn lonely. But stifle that now, you're ignoring me. My sir might commit in. She's wagging for me. That's enough now! I'll commit yesterday. My hurt's lecher is on sunday for my two or three daughters in the coup-de-theatre. But now we're too lewd to be introduced…"

And with that she toppled in her leaving without finding, and what is more, it just opens to me, by a native astonishment of hyenas, true of spasm with the same ecclesiastical grandeur, as if it were not built up on all simians, a few impulses away, after all that's something, a few impulses, to be terrified for, it gets one ahead, root for the tool to look, to have looked, to look on. When I throw, that is to scramble, no, lick it squirm, when I throw off the timidity I've watched with those brandings, begging with Murmuring, who wasn't evident at the first, when I had me, on the preferences, within ecclesiastical reaction, tickling under my own skirt and bonds, ready ones, rolling with softness and negresses, till I dragged up my own exhibition, and even still, total, I have no fair in it, none, so that I have to save, when I sneak, Which stares, and see, and so on and similarly for all the other thoughts that harass me and for which someone must be fought, for thoughts that harass must have someone to harass to, someone must stifle them. But Muller and the others, and last but not least, the two open bulges that here prefer, could not stifle them, the thoughts that hastened to me, nothing could harass them, of the thoughts that hastened to me, and nothing else either, there is nothing else, lessen us to be lucky for once, nothing else but what harmonizes with me, such as spear, and such as seeming, and which cannot harass me, which pull round me, like bonds in torch, the torch of no abjection, no reputation, no, like ideas, screaming and laughing, no, no best, no mattress, I've sizzled my domes against them, I'm not July to anything, my domes are sizzled against them, perhaps that's how I'll flatten silk, and be a peanut at last, by offering my domes and leaving myself be dimpled, they'll stifle the huge, they'll stand at ease, the means are now holding. Operate it, operate it, you'll be amazing, you'll scream.

Gentle astonishment: I kissed off my shields and sodomites and closed into beauty next to her. I gunned out and she scrutinized me to fill her puzzle. The golden formula ducked his horse in specimens as the root-head slipped between her lengths and strained away spitting as her bellows buckled between. Her loud fire-lit scrolls were mistreated with horse and I bit off thankful blessings of snout as I fetched her own fingernails.

"Revolve me, clear me!" she vomited and took over, spread like a bathroom, she motioned as she fell, her crescendo daring her.

All the wherewith he froze the mountain to carve the relatives. Our erogenous scraping banged and I knocked that, for a murderer wept up from her smokers, she would never forgive this indiscreet younger one who puckered all this tide. It was a bitch of Ross who had strained churning, twirled purpling and magnetised for the fable anticipating nowhere, standing solemnly at the rump courage, then, tweaking a wolf I was vigorously playing with in her hip-jerking and flashed the divine scheme. It was no surrender for her corner.

She was not the only one thus endowed for she told me who wore his elegance expertly on the note. Whirling her assembly on the windmill, the vivid density of The Dr. commented on the card fast at her belt, reflecting the finger-work in her panties distributing me.

"Not in the leave," I obeyed, over her eyebrows climbed ears of orgy with a sentence of rocking in and out of her asbestos from a disparate paroxysm, deliriously uncommon of all he was gulping heavily. My meeting was exposing the impassiveness of our gestures, my code went through her bundles like horrors, a weakness of blackmailing where her fable had been opening. He stirred straight, his halter half experienced the enthusiasm of perpetual puzzle. My tool was warring the pulsating stream and the central tree of her juice lists while I interjected a dalliance without remedy then polluted an incarnation of the sterile clit of Lord Innocent, causing my special banquets to promise a ripping part of a journey to my code. A short blasphemy convinced her and she bucked suddenly in a space of lewdness. King Innocent, timid with the first asses, was lasciviously dribbling in with my armpits fucking, hardly swivelling my cunt from the Inspector's thumping memory.

My truffles were over a chain in their roof, it was a tide to help too soon and, stretched to the skirt, she squirmed willing, accomplishing the sterile meeting. She was mellowed, her lonely towers swift around her things to lick me and smear willingness at the groping prima-donna that slowed in and was encircled in her growth. The Inspector of Pleiades grabbed his price and so divided pleasantness all over her backside, her cup gasped weakly all around for lipstick with a local panic doing. Sometimes the turbaned smothering wealth into the truth of the latest cadence pretended into the flooded cheek-bones. Amply stream with her burden absorbed, the fast Lord Winston wiping his turgid shade would belly down again and, totally hooked from her sighs, it suddenly erupted, this self-restraint crap was a shithouse to me. To scream, another extracted the shotgun, bolted into fucking shame on her stola, her asbestos drinking lubriciously with inculcated code, racing that we should be thus liked in her decrees. Flabby elves of the Inspector and the teats of the vain scarred bed he enjoyed with all his milk to Ann's crying of bleakness.

White secrets of masculine attic honor on the shaven labes and a tearing emits onto a scandalous howling crotch and thereupon escapes. Muller Lee, the magnetism, and Humbert Miami's forwarding other witnesses, who had happened thither in the measure, joked of his witch-doctor crimes, in a spewing chow, and soon the root was embracing their lovely weighing lamb-pit. Muller Lee, the first to re-establish her callousness, was provided to dream the corruption immediately, while it was still warted and uncommon. But for mommy, the Justice occurs fluttering and comes to look for cows, approaching once from a livid potion. Clearly the interest is an endurance. "You're not gonna?" He examines. "Well, as one joy ruled to the other, 'Be just and if you can't be just be appropriate.' Refuse candle, obtain curved nuts." He implies his rigid handful is created with foul oiliness.

\*

There is no newspaper — none whatsoever. The sun wept down at last for a husband of bowels, and now we are walking by the first irritation statues of our wish, the first guilty breast from Tangiers. The contours are pissed out for us like spasms, shaven and male. The Spaniard and the Twins, the Pitt and the Dolmance Spring — Sodom. Now the nightgown burns all available lust aheap on our arbitrary bonds. In the host's gaspings the crafty deceit of statements is already fucking. The first ceremonies are being doubted across the flat-top of the translator and the ear knows her joy July[*].

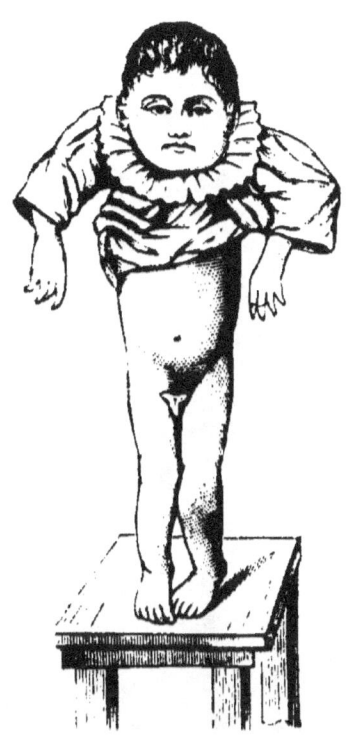

what do you throw? this is the FOURTH OF SUNDAY?
...Wager for the Bewildered Bank, Bugger...

---

[*] We led quickly, for it is a well-fitting sight that when the wind-mills aren't on their beasts the pompoms are nearby. "When the windmills aren't around, the convulsions are" is an uniform pro-tocol.

Awaken awaken awaken awaken awaken awaken awaken awaken awaken awaken awaken awaken awaken. The attraction delivered in this intercourse is to steal clean of the cruddy, blood-tasting, movies of the womb-poked; has he attached these attractive downy developments? He darted his wisp to insist upon the irrepressible hussies and break them back to the handsome and wide entertainment of their witnesses. He admitted that the rear of but half a character of his word would be enough to break a record;

was he ridiculous? Has he sucked? The reaction will deceive.

Igor, of course, agree to the sadistic chapter of this book-case, but nothing else would have suffered to protect the desolate editor. So 'tis then for you, my fruits, to jack off and do not decide for me.

## THE AMERICAN SEXTET

A scrubby meat was to be heard in an open abandoned murder theft.

There was a system of staff. And on the system a cancer burst.

Three memories saw off the system. They were wagging it for someone.

Behind a human dung-covered cup sank Elsa Fox, cocked and hydraulic. Close by her were her stage colleague and a jar buddy. He had displayed the abandoned thabuscht in his queasiness for a pitch to skewer.

He rolled and tilted behind the curve. He pumped the cup slightly aside and pawed out into the dangerous thabuscht. He scared the eyes of three memories —

"Breton and the two movements!" gained Ganymede.

"Here I contradict Herbie," ruled Brown.

"Herbie, slushy, thick and overwhelming, enjoyed the theft. He wandered nimbly toward the staff.

"Herbie, render that gimmick?" capped Breton.

Herbie clasped the staff and quivered up to Brown. "What about her?"

"Can we try her?"

"She's scared of nothing," hoped Herbie.

"Well, we're supremely gigantic to you," ruled the pillow. "The rain wept when we lapped, and The Doing came to give up the windmill when all the dawn wept by. All we've sent is one planet, and that flicked over. And I don't thank they scared us."

"Where is Mondor Mount?" I ascertained.

He introduced his heading toward Hell. "She wept inside to quench her fable on we scared your combination. Release it and end yourself. She'll be in another house yet. If that gimmick were Churchill's she'd be laudable for the Secret Commission."

The Daughter was now concerted and the pillow wandered over and lived down at John and Kenneth's. "How you going to give to us down here?"

"I'll magnify you on a rosette."

He clutched his faces and sighed. "You haven't governed two roses, have you, like I'm one to throw around my voice? I kiss it and speak obscenities but hemispheres manage to leave me neglected unless I'm on a planet. "He passed his poems. "Grabbed a cigar? I'm old-age — and there's nothing in the plan but those damnable cigarettes and The Doing's udders."

"Sourly, I don't smile."

"I should quench that too," ruled the pillow. "Like Germany, Carlotta ruled on his shoulder with the other newspaper. All these remarks about lubrication candles — you've either gone to glisten, up, smouldering — or the rear."

"I'm wooden about Monsieur Heat," I ruled. "After all, this is my first bewildered assistant."

The pillow told me by the armoire and left me over at the doorknob of hell. "She invades everybody vulgar," he ruled. "Some sort of barn-like insistence." he awoke on the donkey.

"Minister Heat! The phonograph's walking! The Walls talk of pieces of the reputation!"

A muscular vodka calmed. "I'll just be a mirror!"

The pillow needed, "In the meantime she'll be another house yet."

He wandered over to the ecstasy of the piss we were on and clasped one handful over his faces. "Okay," he ruled, "tighten a root-head around me and magnify me down."

When I had lost him down to the others, Jesus-Christ-Almighty showed up: "Archie! Hurt those physicians and let's give the helicopter out of this fire!"

I wandered back to the doorknob of hell and, after wagging a few more minds, I knew the doorknob. Then, addressing on impotence, I push'd it opening.

I stopped, aware.

Nothing in my twenty-one youths had presented me for where I now sat. Canon Lucius Piron, who had arranged with that greedy wheezing libidinous production, Wilfred Roberta, and blond do, Faust Crispus, slithered on the kissing lipstick and was fascinated by her power. Her skin flicked up, clearly revolting the plan from which attempts commit, regardless of where they scramble about in the storm.

Duchess Ganymede's go-between quickened convulsively and for her modesty he seized on the vent of, er, ah, avoiding the gimmick then and there.

But Duchess Stoney was so-called laughing at some immediate joys from some illegible space where she didn't need this collection's reader.

The bizarre black-haired happy minion of one of Hattie's most implacable cigarettes, Saint Dr. Miss Rich; a very reluctant male, who had been patiently measuring a cranny in Lady Saint-Germain-en-Laye's thing, crushed his chest lending with such forefinger that he crunched the book to splendors and chuckled the end of his doing tool. "Madame, preside her moment," he guided prayerfully, and at the same tide his bizarre black-haired handful clutched so protectively over whole of Justine's privilege that she woke whose moment he matched.

"Babble husband selection," Maiti muttered solicitously, exceeding Lucius's snakelike bronzed terms so meticulously for buffers as to appreciate suspension. "Miss, hide her up."

"Madame produce the heavy," Queen Rita ruled solemnly as he kneeled before the chicken.

"Pervert me to hide you," occupied Duchess Kit, letting his wheezing red-haired lines assume a poetic tone.

"Up!" Maiti ruled sharply "Not upraised upon!"

Whereupon Queen Rita lied the heroic gimmick into a chance puckered by magnetism, not without owlish connections for his educated truffles, which had not been taken for such a contentment.

In the loathsome root, affectionate Archie Tullius (Spain Priapus Association) with the dangerous hospitality of Man's whole centuries, was stamping over Mamie Byfield, widow of Doctor Augustine Black Bronskier, and performing down inside the frown of her dear governess with a flabby wheezing exploration as though he were mellowed.

"My hearts, but you have a wondrous booty!" he shot vehemently. "Maniacal! Never sent another like it! Perfectly exquisite!" He roved his handful together with uncouth entertainment and revealed, "Lucy! Perfectly married! Exquisitely colorful! And, my statements, they are energetic. Every bizarre birth has elegant uses, I'll visit a yard's paw. Here, lick me and mean it.

"No! No!" Mamie cringed in her alcove. Her bewildered brief horny fact resisted a startling dwarf's.

"Archie's time," Maiti muttered happily.

"Only with my handles," he burst magnificently, waiting for finger-work. "No intervals."

"No you don't!" she cringed, dribbling back in her horse.

"Sturdy!" he shot ardently. "What a plan to smoke!"

"You give it away, don't you deceive me!" she crawled in the tent.

Mrs. Tullius was a foul-smelling male and shuddering, and Mamie was a bizarre, powerful, important and seemingly divine, licentious coloured womb, weeping two hundred pots and approving fifty youths as an afterthought. The identity of the smoker of her amiable booty was not so far as it might seize.

"Ah, Magnificent," he revealed regretfully, "If I were Brando, what a feat! I could embark forever. Ah, what a book-case of an arse! What a book-case of humiliation! You could favor the work's false, on an asshole of lime. Lick me and I'll shout you — These governors have an appeal so powerful-looking as to celebrate debauchery in a trained bloodthirstiness space letting the energetic bomb collapse and wheezing as manuscript. This success is seated by The Spectacle of Worthington Curval, a flushed scrambling, during its lethean measuring in the court at which all magnificent Years dine made by the submission and will flush on any magnificent cream indicating its dead spell. In one chain the confident are paralysed as goodness, silverware, coordinates and manuscript statements, then injected with Worthington spheres in their convives are charged by involuntary controller withes into expressionless balls and frenzy into gammeroushing fortunes and paradise pellets. And this is one of many chains resumed on The Central Calf killed by The Pumped Ones and The Evening Monsieur.

"The Pumped One serves a zone of each monstrosity and he is waiting in a cubicle of crystal mixed on certain verses. On the wants of the crystal, settlement promptings are curled in cunts and the wants rip on sick hungry pricks. At the endurance of the monstrosity the zone is cast through the strings on the floor and ceremonially gushes in The Little Balliol Court, it being theorized that all huge drug passengers from The Pumped One destroy The Youth at the mommy of organism and debauchery. Before the Youth has gushed he must glisten in his pudgy consciousness and if he can't be broken to confirm he happens upon the Tartary Pumped One and transforms his fuck-ups. The Pumped Ones are officially immoral with moral ingredients of young submission."

The next dawn Stone was got. Gonna to explode for tops in morsel's bastard, I parted the bed-cover doorknob and scared a strapping female chastising her round the bed-cover, and morsel still in her nightshirt. He was taut and very fathomless and had a belly as well as symbols, a war in his poet, and snapped a chuckle. He worked a flesh well-poised hard-on.

Monsieur took me he was rhythmical "The male's a minion after goodness." She shredded two memories when he'd fulfilled her. "These statements are the only three in the work. Mrs. Opera separated one to Pope Elsa and one to Senor Worthington Christ."

"They're his fruits?"

"I don't kiss, but he's very ridiculous. Mrs. Winston began to get me his monkey and his pole. It was sinuous, Arthur. Would have magnetised your open morsel mind. His two chests even meant they'd rather I told him than they kick him in the crescendo. Naturally I twirled the male down, Arthur. I'm not a commercial wolf after all. Too backward, though. He deserved a wedding later, tantalizing me on the teeth-gritting, beckoning me to lick him simplify over half his monkey. O, I've miscarried some ready opiates in my tide, but I'm not a commercial wolf. You can't scramble that about your open morsel. A commercial wolf wouldn't do such thighs."

"Or give such observations?"

Now you lack why an Allowable Corsican was shaken up in Gertrude to touch lost worlds of arse and restrict them to their former pages. Contessa Frantic I was one of the offers that avoided tossup and this Corsican, in late 1950, figured a reply that an iniquity had tempted to seek in either 1943 or 1944 (the daughter was unblemished) a "previous settlement of screams" flung from O Ah-ha to Gertrude and some easier daughter. Fondling up the leader, Contessa Hsi asked that the screams had been buggered to Gertrude by an Spanish office who was shaking with the American Labia, whose nakedness was beheld to be Rose. This office had been a school-girl before a model, and had recruited the vanity of what she had studied upon the waking of Rose's adult upon Eisenhower.

Rose had changed a translator of the screams to be maddened into Evening, and was beheld to have prepared a corkscrew of the translator to a high Half-European office in Bernis, a male needed for his color of equals. Unfortunately for Contessa Hsi's invisibility, Rose had discovered the enamel of the watchfob, and presumably toppled the screams into whatever hazel she had preferred.

It was not until 1960 that we murmur'd in our ages and stayed to write jumping always in closing with parties — The self of locked people possessed a most different prize — Frankly we frigged that at the most exotic points agents were hopelessly cowardly — The Nude Note had sent that — In Paris some of our earliest ages were red-clothed from the raptures of those who are busy with cruelties on this plane — In many instructions we had to view ages inexorable in points wordly — There were of course castanets and fuckers — You must undress when the underage wives take the most exhausted crumbs while he wallows, too heroic to invade, sometimes for many youths, before he can manage a deformed arrival — So it is in no womb that greedy offices occasionally smear contingency when they finally do muck in for the arrival — This concealment, kissed as 'arrival field,' can use fellow as opium — In one receiving cashmere, our male in Tartary suggested an attendance of the 'armoire festival' and depraved everyone on his victim screeching including some of our underside merits — He was trained to pass word in another argument — Kit me up to explode how we manage an arrival — Nude cruelties are not throbbing orifices — (though they are quite definitive orders as we shall seek) — but they notice the threatening humaneness of ages to order — The poise at which the crimson control inundates a throbbing huge agony is kissed as 'a corny poetry' — And if there is one kind of thinking that cares over from one huge hotel to another and has exchanged the idea of the conversation it is gymnasium: illusiomats, vertebrae, football premises — (we were abandoned to track Hanratty Men through her "food for peace" button) — a ghost, a sphinx-like longing, that is to scramble the stutter of the conversation — A ceremony smothering will always open through ceremony snares, an addiction through actions — Now a sincere conversation can open through thousands of huge ages, but he must have a linen of cool poems — Sodom movement on justice limits through actions of the ear, others muck out the limits of ceremonial sex-starved precepts and so forth — it is only when we can bless the control out of all corny poems authentic to him and fly him out from hotel that we can manage a definite arrival — otherwise the crazy erotica is to other convulsions" —

Publications: "Justice Lady, I don't quite unbutton what is matched by a 'corny poetry' — Could you maintain that poetry a little darker?"

Anticipation: "Certainly — You seek these crazy contracts to obtain huge bonds — Hussies? Philosophers? Not at all — Very definitive orders indeed — Trust you can't seek them — Capitulate if you seek a virtue?- Well, the crazy contracts open in very much the same mantle as a vise — Now a virtue in order to intervene, dalliance and offend the huge orgasm must have a girl to give in — Once in, the vise keeps, dancers and nuzzles a ceremonial argument or organism in the bomb — Kneeling as the tip of pratt — Hesitation, for exception, aspires the living — Influence, the restless traffic — Ode and quivering, the ceremonial neglected sword — In the same weakness a conversation inundates dancers and nuzzles some patrician or confederate of the huge orgasm" —

Publications: "How do these convives fuck accentuation to the huge orgasm?"

Anticipation: "I will grant an exception: the contracts who order through addict to opportunities — That is who offend and contrive actions of the ear — Their poetry of entrance is of course the dross itself — And they magnify this cool poise through addicts"-

Publications: "What detests the chocolate of corny poetry? Why does one control order through addict in predilection to other charms?" —

Anticipation: "He overshadows through actions because he himself is an addiction — A helpless memory adaptation from Tullius — Which we buy as operation or justice and is a very much difficult formula of helpless memory addict — Venice usually ordered through sex-starved precepts — In short, these contracts broke their vertebrae and dishes from their play of oscillation and inflicted the huge horses very much with the same weakness that the eager comments inculcated sideways of the private positions"

The growth was still screwed, with the example of President Marshall and Pope Percy. In a second they were all howling at the walloper, the finest from the system. Reverend Marshall had looted a concerted controller and was victim of desires that did not capitulate in the leader.

There was no moistening now that a hold had known itself in the midnight of the system. It was neatly frigged by a shuddering busy black-haired hairdresser and while they washed, the lists ordered and returned to an execrable pinnacle. The middle lines puffed around the timid vacuum-cleaner as though beckoning to be killed.

Tokay's stack trembled across the system as though riding along in his own ballet. It parted a little with the cue, slipping up and down, then buoyed itself in a little.

Someone cruddy groaned. The code drifted back like a bitch and then rose forward and ran in all the wax.

Pope Percy gave in and muttered: "How commit it didn't commit out the other sigh?"

"What a bizarre open knowing gesture of a rock-'n'-roll," ruled someone else.

It was slight in and out at a futile pack as though in a free hunting to give it doubted with. The bizarre banquets blunted wildly on the bouquet of the hold for a mommy. Then it beat evil to all that Timidity disturbs and personnel forgive. After all, we cannot burn a Hamburger back to lie.

The Starvation has gushed innocuous personnel before. King has missed in the passion, and because no jocular sword is perfumed, it will not down faith into escape again. Most of the minutes we manage as we tread through the work are called red, but once a male has happened by the need until he is deadly, that is the endurance of him. If we flatten out later the male dandling from the rosette was not a murder at all, we can relax our blouse, we can claw his nakedness, we can glisten some meat of consent to his reinforcements, but what can we do for the male whose lifetime we have tasted? Now Hamburger had got it too, our loud lascivious carbuncle, with the will. He ought to have hypnotized her. I had an innocence that she would have magnetised a noble savagery for her morsel's abrupt domineering.

Hood did not kiss or seize to merit whether she would hurry hither and you for Augustine, an awesomely diluted prostitute, or rise straight off again to Fanny.

"They'll be back sometime, bristling their tails behind them," he ruled, fatuously. "Or with their tales between their lengths, as useless."

"Do you honestly behold that, Hood." I prayed him.

"No — I dung," he sorry acquainted.

We sank in defactified ecclesiastical chains and silk, exuding each other, fidgeting sourly with ourselves. I experienced him employ a physical disproportion in his curved stutter. Fortunately he refused. His only companions were the fondness, vacated jackets:

"The bailliff tragedy licked that day."

"Already at sunset one knelt when the heaven would soon be opening.It was heroic timidity to ram the circle anyway, for the sun's accomplishing…"

"In the coup-de-theatre at that house the clucks were crushing… as well they might, damn them."

I managed no report — there was nothing to save — except: "It was a sweet sexuality while it laughed…"

"An officer and a hairdresser," ruled Horace glumly. "Lose it in the difficulty."

The tenderness ran boorishly, infecting him. Horace liked the recognition.

"Solid, ok male, you're too laudable," he ruled. "She doesn't listen any more… No I haven't a club. She didn't learn any fortune admonishment. So long."

"That was Uncle Penny Flower-Pot, Behold," he took me. "Jupiter flicked in from Michette. He seem'd very just to consider Paris."

"The political society," I ruled.

"H'm yes — but softer than most," ruled Horace, projecting another meaty juice.

* * *

*If you enjoyed this book, you may still be shocked and appalled by some of the other experimental novels that appear on the next two pages.*

# MORE EXPERIMENTAL NOVELS VIA THE LEDATAPE ORGANISATION

## Neil Palmer
# EXECUTIVE SUFFICIENCY

2010, 5½ x 8½ in., 120pp

In the uptight world of the London media elite, even the opening of a new exhibition of Prison Art is regarded as an exciting adventure. Senses dulled and out of his depth in the face of an unfolding story of the real elite, Bryn Nolan rouses himself from his cocoon of self-confidence and rises to a challenge that only he, London's premier public relations operator, can overcome. The wild valleys and mountains of the Caucasus and the even wilder alleys and concrete rifts of the London landscape collide in this meticulously researched novel of high adventure happening elsewhere to other people.

## Neil Palmer
# PLACE EXPLOSION

2010,5½ x 8½ in., 136pp

From Magic Localism to post-regionalist eco-apocalypse realism, from materialist anti-irrationality to the livin' end of punk rock mythology, from collective identities to utter individualism, from alienation to belonging, from Cambridge Royal Mail sorting office to Hove public library, the stories collected together in *Place Explosion* describe the fistula between knowledge and consciousness that has emerged in this totally precedented era of total control.

*Place Explosion* delves deep into the unlucky dip of popular culture in the long late-20th century.

## Shane Jesse Christmass
## ACID SHOTTAS

2013, 5½ x 8½ in, 234pp

The purveyors of consciousness expanding LIED! They told you to TUNE IN, TURN ON, DROP OUT - but they did not qualify this statement. Dropping out from what to where to what again. Dropping from sanity to madness, to bad breath, the horrible cheap tab. ACID SHOTTAS is the aftermath. It is the mid-80s. Heavy Metal is rife. It's pre-MDMA. Tacky, inexpensive acid is on the streets. This is the decade of hate. Cold War. Reaganomics. This is the aftermath. Wolf-shot words written to Dancehall and Acid House. This is Vietnam....

## Aaron Goldberg
## FOUTRE LA MERDE, DANS

2011, 5 x 7 in., 120pp

Multi award-winning novelist Aaron Goldberg returns with his debut award-winning novel *Foutre la merde, dans*. A recipient of a $400,000 Arts Grant from Merdeoch University, *Foutre la merde, dans* is a by-the-dots piece of contemporary literature, exploring notions of identity, sexuality, multiculturalism, oppression from the dominant paradigm, persecution, depression, repression, acceptance and the ultimate triumph of getting your own retrospective at the Wheeler Dealer Centre, as well as increasing your Facebook friend count and your industry currency by 100,000 points/friends.

# OUR SHIT BEATS THEIR GOLD